The Pantheon Fairy Tale and Folklore Library

African Folktales by Roger D. Abrahams

African American Folktales by Roger D. Abrahams

American Indian Myths and Legends by Richard Erdoes and Alfonso Ortiz

Arab Folktales by Inea Bushnaq

Chinese Fairy Tales and Fantasies by Moss Roberts

The Complete Grimm's Fairy Tales by Jacob and Wilhelm Grimm

Favorite Folktales from Around the World by Jane Yolen

Folktales from India by A.K. Ramanujan

French Folktales by Henri Pourrat

Gods and Heroes by Gustav Schwab

Irish Folktales by Henry Glassie

Japanese Tales by Royall Tyler

Legends and Tales of the American West by Richard Erdoes

The Norse Myths by Kevin Crossley-Holland

Northern Tales by Howard Norman

Norwegian Folk Tales by Peter Asbjørnsen and Jørgen Moe

Russian Fairy Tales by Aleksandr Afanas'ev

Swedish Folktales and Legends
by Lone Thygesen Blecher and George Blecher

The Victorian Fairy Tale Book by Michael Patrick Hearn

Chinese Fairy Tales and Fantasies

Chinese Fairy Tales and Fantasies

Translated and edited by Moss Roberts

With the assistance of C. N. Tay

Pantheon Books
New York

Library of Congress Cataloging in Publication Data
Main entry under title:

Chinese fairy tales and fantasies.

1. Fantastic fiction, Chinese—Translations into English.
2. Fantastic fiction, English—Translations from Chinese.
3. Fairy tales, Chinese—Translations into English. 4. Fairy tales, English—Translations from Chinese. I. Roberts, Moss, 1937–
PL2658.E8C48   895.1'3'008   79-1894
ISBN 0-394-73994-9

Manufactured in the United States of America

68C97

Design by Irva Mandelbaum

For Sean and Jennifer

Contents

Acknowledgments

I would like to thank first of all Professor C. N. Tay of New York University for his sustaining encouragement and for sharing his extraordinary knowledge of language and literature;

the Pantheon editor, Wendy Wolf, and the copy editor, Mary Barnett, whose excellent judgment in matters of literary taste and English style improved my manuscript in countless ways;

my wife, Florence, and my children, Sean and Jennifer, who read the manuscript with care and made many valuable suggestions;

our friend, Shirley Hochhausen, who listened to these tales with a keen and appreciative ear;

the students in the East Asian Studies Program at New York University, who have stimulated so much of my research into Chinese literature.

A Note on the Illustrations

The illustrations were taken from the Ming encyclopedia *San Ts'ai T'u Huei*, or *Compendium of Illustrations for the Three Orders of Heaven, Earth, and Man* (1608). I am grateful to Mr. Jack Jacoby of the East Asian Collections of the Columbia University Libraries for permission to use their reprint edition. I also wish to thank Mr. David Tsai, Curator, and Ms. Alice Chi of the Gest Oriental Library of Princeton University for their assistance.

Introduction

The tales, fables, and fantasies in this collection blend the every-day life of mortals, the fabulous kingdom of birds and beasts, and the supernatural world of gods and ghosts. Like Western folk and fairy tales, they spring from the deep wells of a civilization's history and imagination, and their cast of peasants, philosophers, virgins, kings, judges, tigers, and parrots may sometimes remind us of characters in more familiar legends. At the same time, these stories bear the stamp of the society and traditions that originally produced them. They illuminate the Chinese social order through the structured relationships that defined it: emperor and subject, father and son, husband and wife (or wives), official and peasant, human and beast.

The Confucian philosophers who dominated the Chinese state conceived these relationships as a harmonious balance of obligations, and a number of pieces in this collection illustrate their view of order and authority. By and large, the Confucians were the voice of the superior orders—emperor, father, husband. The majority of our tales, however, speak for the other side, for they come from the Taoists, philosophers and social critics who represented the subordinate orders and historically opposed the Confucians. The Taoist view found vivid expression in popular literature—novels, plays, and the tales and legends we read here. Indeed, one of the purposes of this genre, typically scorned and even banned by Confucian authorities, was to publicize the crimes of the mighty and the injustices suffered by the subordinate order, including children, women, and animals. As the conflict between those above and those below gave shape to Chinese history, the rivalry of these two great philosophies gave shape to Chinese culture.

In Confucian doctrine, the emperor sat at the center of the

political, social, and natural realms. He ruled with a mandate from heaven, and his spiritual authority radiated outward in concentric circles; he received in return the allegiance of humans and the submission of creatures and things. The Chinese saw him as both Son of Heaven and father of the people, thus fusing the Western roles of king and pope into a single, semi-divine figure. As the descendant of the founder of his own dynasty, the emperor had charge of the filial worship of his ancestors and the wise governance of his own family—in particular the careful arrangement of marriages and the proper education of the son who would succeed him. In Confucianism, the hereditary principle was foremost, because the imperial family was the heart of the state.

The emperor transmitted his influence across the land directly through the imperial bureaucracy and indirectly through the great landowning clans, sometimes called the local gentry or nobility. Official positions (the goal for every clan's sons) were obtained through a series of qualifying examinations based on the sacred books of Confucian doctrine, ritual, ethics, metaphysics, and history. An ambitious young man could rise by passing three successive levels of examinations, the county, the provincial, and the metropolitan. Each of the degrees brought its holder various immunities, exemptions, and privileges, though not always an actual office. The system was designed to delegate the responsibilities of government to upright and learned men, to scholar-officials who would rule with judgment.

However, these tales deal with practice, not theory, and in reality the bureaucracy was a cumbersome, often corrupt structure in which official appointment was determined by a mixture of factors that included patronage and bribery as well as scholarship. A tale like "The Scholar's Concubine" is meant as a scathing satire on the sale of office to the unqualified.

The official that appears most frequently in this collection is the county magistrate, the lowest official of the imperial bureaucracy and the direct governor of the people in his jurisdiction. He usually held a "metropolitan" or "provincial" degree, and was addressed as "parent of the county." Even so, he was usually a sorry caretaker of the peasants' fortunes, and rarely loved. "A Wise Judge" and "A Clever Judge" pay tribute to good magistrates; but "Social Connections" tells how a vicious official ruins a prosperous farmer, and "Underworld Justice" goes further to show how little justice there is in this world or the next.

The closing selection of this book, chapter one of the eighteenth-century novel *An Unofficial History of the Confucian Academy*, satirizes the entire official realm. In it, the hero, Wang Mien, refuses to take office despite his enormous talents and the wishes of the emperor, taking to heart his mother's dying wish: "Take a wife and raise a family; care for my grave—and don't become an official." Such criticism rarely touched the emperor himself. An exception is the opening tale, "The Cricket," in which the whole bureaucracy mobilizes to cater to the court's newest fad.

The great clans ruled locally, little models of the imperial family. Here too, hereditary right was enforced to assure the smooth transmission of property and status; and to that end the arrangement of marriages was essential. If a young noble and his first wife had little choice in the matter, secondary wives or concubines had none at all. Generally speaking, in a society that makes the family a political as well as a social unit, freedom of love and marriage cannot be tolerated; personal preference and appetite must be overruled by the social virtues. The response to this demand—the struggle for freedom to love and marry—became the spark in much of Chinese literature, as we see in "The Divided Daughter," which describes with compassion the sorrow of couples who want to marry for love, not duty, and in "The Waiting Maid's Parrot," where a young concubine who loves a scholar finds that help can come from an unusual source.

The control of emotion lies at the heart of the Confucian's perception of human nature. The Confucians defined human beings solely in terms of a set of obligatory relationships, in which the essence, the fundamental act, was obedience: children obeyed parents, peasants obeyed lords and officials, wives obeyed husbands. This was the primary force in behavior—leaving passion and instinct as attributes not of humans but of animals; we encounter an official who has fallen into this savage state in "The Censor and the Tiger."

Master storyteller P'u Sung-ling, who sets the dominant tone in this volume, attacks this entire tradition in a set of tales in which animals and other "subordinate" creatures set the standards for virtuous conduct that their superiors would do well to follow; in "The Loyal Dog," "The Snakeman," and "A Faithful Mouse," he shows eloquently where love and compassion are truly demonstrated. Twenty-one of the tales here come from P'u's *Record of Things Strange in a Makeshift Studio*, a collection of over four hundred tales which is the culmination of the Chinese short-story tradition. The manuscript of this work was probably completed toward the end of the seventeenth century and circulated widely, though it was not formally published until the 1760s, some fifty years after P'u's death.

The literary countertradition of which P'u may be the principal figure has its roots in Taoism, a philosophy as old as Confucianism and the one most consistently critical of it. Tao (literally "the way" or "the main current") is the universal ancestor and the universal annihilator. As the ultimate leveler of all living creatures, it creates all things equal, giving no one of them dominion over another by virtue of birth or any other inheritable power. Tao's authority is absolute; it transfers no authority to what it creates—quite unlike the Confucian heaven, which gives its "son" the emperor a mandate to rule. As destroyer, Tao gathers up again all it has produced; none of its myriad creatures can transfer influence, property, or status beyond its ordained time. Animals and all other creatures exist on the same level as humans, and each exists for one lifetime alone, free of obligations to either ancestors or descendants. According to the Taoists, the artifices of civilization only lead people away from the original and benign state of nature. Thus at one blow the Taoists shattered the fundamental premise of the Confucian order: the social hierarchy founded on hereditary right.

More than twenty pieces in this collection come from the great Taoist philosophers Chuang Tzu and Lieh Tzu. Two brief selections, "The Fish Rejoice" and "Butterfly Dreams," imagine how the human and animal realms are part of the same whole. Chuang Tzu, in particular, sought a state of personal transcendence in which the spirit would be free to rove among the entirety of creation, becoming one first with this, then with that. This interplay between the human and animal worlds connects Taoism to the Buddhists, who believed that the spirits of the dead may reappear in animal form to atone for the sins of previous lifetimes. The transmigration of souls figures dramatically in "Suited to Be a Fish" and "Three Former Lives." Both tales also teach the importance of compassion toward all living things, the essence of Buddhist ethics.

The humanization of animals in these tales reflects yet another cultural association: the relations between the Chinese and the non-Chinese. Confucian historians were often outraged by the marriage and burial customs of the innumerable Asian peoples, some non-Chinese, some partly Chinese, who lived around China's borders. Concerned with preserving the purity of Chinese ethnic and cultural identity, the Confucians often referred to these peoples with unflattering animal names like "hound" and "reptile." The Taoists and Buddhists, on the other hand, had a far more tolerant view. Lieh Tzu's "Man or Beast" voices this challenge in a powerful way, recognizing in mythic terms the contributions non-Chinese peoples had made to Chinese civilization.

But the Taoists did not deal only in imaginative metaphors. The Taoist priests whose magical powers are displayed throughout the tales spurned the teachings of the Confucian classics and the careers of bureaucrats in order to study alchemy, astrology, botany, pharmacology, meteorology, zoology, and so forth. Rebels as often as recluses, they lived in the mountains where tigers reigned and outlaws hid. As critics of the social order, they often joined the peasants in resisting and at times overthrowing the dynasty in power, thus translating their egalitarian view of creation into social and economic reality. Antidynastic movements such as the White Lotus (a society of peasant rebels active from the twelfth century to the nineteenth) often made use of the "heresies" and "black arts" the Taoists taught them. "White Lotus Magic" and "The Peach Thief" afford us a glimpse of their activities.

The Confucian social order was threatened from yet another source, the supernatural world. In the Confucian view, the dead commanded an authority that could be invoked only in the ancestral temple, and only by their living—and noble—descendants. These rituals had enormous social and psychological influence over the common people, whose untitled and often homeless dead were silent and impotent. A rival and contemporary of Confucius, the philosopher Mo Tzu, devised an ingenious way to reverse this concept. Ghosts, Mo argued, are not the agents of the privileged living; rather, they are agents of heaven. As the collective common dead, they are the enforcers of a universal, objective justice and can compensate for the defects in human justice. The City God who plays an important role in "Underworld Justice" is criticized for neglecting this duty. The City God had a public temple in the city which gave anyone who entered and sought it access to the world of the dead. The local deity in "Drinking Companions" is a variant of the same idea. Many of the other tales in the section *Ghosts and Souls* poke fun at those who believe in ghosts that are creations of mere superstition, not agents of justice.

These, then, are a few of the social themes that come into play as the tales unfold. Together the collection spans over twenty centuries of Chinese literature, from the fifth century B.C. to the eighteenth A.D. Yet each tale has its own voice, speaking to us with vivid honesty of common feelings about human life.

TALES OF ENCHANTMENT AND MAGIC

❧ The Cricket

During the Ming reign known as Pervasive Virtue cricket fighting was very popular at court, and each year the populace had to supply crickets for the noblemen to test in battle. In Floral Shade, our county in western Shensi, the cricket is not common. But our magistrate wanted to curry favor with his superiors, and he managed to find them one that proved to be a mighty warrior. As a result Floral Shade was appointed a royal supplier of crickets to the court.

Naturally the magistrate then shifted the responsibility down to the neighborhood heads, and crickets became rare and valuable in the county. In hopes of pushing the price up, the young bloods in our towns often hoarded the outstanding specimens they caught. Cunning local officials were quick to use cricket hoarding as an excuse for searching people's houses. And whenever they looked for cricket collections, they confiscated so many other goods that they ruined several families at a time.

In Floral Shade there lived a man called Make-good. He had spent years as a candidate for the lowest degree, but it still eluded him. Make-good was somewhat pedantic and unassertive, and crafty officials maneuvered him into the post of neighborhood head. Once there, he was stuck in the job; a hundred schemes and tricks would not have extricated him. When he could not extort enough taxes from the people, he had to make up the money out of his own pocket. Within a year the whole of his property was exhausted.

The same thing happened when it came time to collect crickets: Make-good could not bring himself to take them from his neigh-

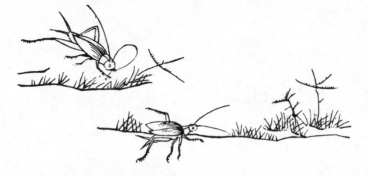

bors, even though he could not fill the quota set by the higher-ups. Trapped in this frustrating situation, he wanted to die.

"What good will dying do?" his wife asked. "Go out and look for crickets yourself. Maybe you'll have some luck."

To this Make-good agreed, and day after day he left home early and returned late. Carrying his bamboo tube and brass wire cage, he searched among crumbling walls and clumps of wild grass. He probed every rock and flushed every hole, but nothing came of it. Although he managed to find a few specimens, they were inferior and weak, far below the standard.

The magistrate, however, held Make-good strictly to schedule. After ten days the unlucky man could furnish no crickets and had to face the punishment of one hundred strokes. He was beaten until the blood ran down both legs and he could not have moved to catch a simple worm. Tossing on his bed, he wished only to make an end of himself.

It happened then that a hunchbacked fortune teller who could read the future came to the village. Make-good's wife took some money for a fee and went to consult her. Crowds thronged the fortune teller's door; Make-good's wife entered the house along with the rosy-cheeked, the grey, and the old. Low incense tables stood in front of an inner chamber screened by curtains. Those who had come with questions were lighting their incense for the crucibles and offering their respects with low bows that ended with the forehead pressed to the floor. The fortune teller stood to one side staring at the sky and chanting to bring the assembled multitude good luck. Her lips opened and closed but formed no intelligible words. The crowd listened with reverent attention. Every few minutes a piece of paper, bearing words that spoke perfectly to a petitioner's concern, would slip out of the curtained chamber.

Make-good's wife placed her money on the stand and performed the same obeisance as her predecessors. In the time it takes to have a meal, the curtains began to quiver and then issued a slip of paper, which fell to the floor. It bore not a single word but only a picture: a sketch of a neglected shrine behind which a small mountain rose from grotesque rocks. The rocks rested amid clumps of vegetation, and a prize greenhead cricket lurked there. Beside it was a frog that seemed about to leap and dance.

Puzzled, the woman scrutinized the picture inch by inch. When her eyes came to rest on the cricket, she gazed with rapt attention, folded the paper, and went home to show it to her husband.

Make-good examined it and mused: "This has to be a way of telling me where to catch a cricket!" He looked long at the scene. It reminded him of a Buddhist temple east of the village. Painfully he arose, supporting himself on his staff, and hobbled with sketch in hand to the temple. At the rear of the building were many ancient graves, and he threaded his way through them. In one spot, strangely shaped rocks appeared virtually as the sketch showed. Alert, cautious, searching minutely, he pushed farther into the thicket. There was neither trace nor echo of what he had come for, but he groped onward.

Then a frog leaped out of the bushes. Make-good was stunned. He swiftly followed it, and the frog dove into the grass. Right behind, Make-good parted the clump of grass and stared. An insect was crouching at the base. He pounced; it slipped into a crevice of the rocks. He tickled it with a sharp blade of grass but could not make it come out. At last he flushed it with the bamboo tube, and the bug appeared, a magnificent specimen. Make-good pursued and caught it. The insect had a large body and a long tail. Its neck was a dark green, its wings the color of gold.

Elated, Make-good caged the cricket and returned home, where his whole family rejoiced as if he had brought great treasure. They placed the cricket in a tub, fed it all kinds of grain, and guarded it against the time when Make-good would have to meet his next quota.

Now, Make-good had a nine-year-old son, who stealthily uncovered the cricket's tub one day when his father was out. Up the bug leaped and was gone like a shot, so swift that no man could have caught it. By the time the desperate boy hunted it down and trapped it under his hand, a leg was torn off and its belly was split. Moments later, it died. The boy cried out in panic. Then he told his mother, and her face turned deathly pale. "Evil Karma!" she swore. "Now comes the day of ruin! When your father gets home he'll settle with you!" The boy left in tears.

Shortly the father returned, and when his wife told him what had happened he felt as if he had been drenched with ice and snow. In a rage he looked for the boy, but the child was gone without a trace. Afterward they found him in the well.

The father's rage was turned to grief. He pounded the ground and cried out; his one wish was for his own death. Husband and wife were desperate and desolate. Their cottage sent up no smoke. Silently they regarded one another—they had nothing to live for.

As dusk approached they took the boy to be buried. Yet when they caressed him there was a slight sign of breathing. Overjoyed, they laid him on the bed. As the night wore on, the child seemed to revive. Husband and wife took comfort. But the boy's vital spirits did not rally; his breathing was low and suppressed, as if he wanted to sleep. Then Make-good turned to look at the empty cage and was again overcome by despair over the lost cricket. He could give no further thought to his son.

Make-good still lay awake, stiff with anxiety, when the sun carried the day up from the east. Suddenly he heard the crackling chirp of an insect outside. He bolted upright and went to look. There was a cricket, very large! Elated, he tried to catch it, but it leaped away abruptly, chirping as it gained speed. Then Make-good succeeded in cupping his hand over it. He could feel nothing tickling his palm, however, and decided that the cricket had gotten away. But when he lifted his hand, the bug shot out again, and Make-good followed swiftly. He turned a corner—only to lose the insect forever.

Make-good stayed where he was, looking all around, until he spied another cricket crouching on the wall. However, it turned out to be short and small, black and red in color—nothing like the one he had lost. Make-good inspected it indecisively for a moment and then resumed the search for the other cricket. But the bug on the wall dove down between his lapel and his sleeve. It had a shape like a mole cricket, wings like plum blossoms, a squarish head, and long legs. Thinking that after all it might have possibilities, Make-good decided to keep it.

He caged the cricket and took good care of it, though he was afraid that it might not please the authorities. Then an idea struck him: he would test the creature in combat first. He sent for a young wag of the village who had a cricket named Crabshell Green which daily won the local matches. At the sight of Make-good's cricket the wag suppressed a laugh, brought out his own, and placed it in a cage beside the other. Flustered, Make-good stared at the long, imposing Crabshell Green. "What a miserable insect I have raised," thought Make-good. "It will never amount to anything. But I might as well risk it, if only for laughs." So he put his cricket into the tub for combat.

Make-good's small cricket crouched and did not move, like a

warrior steeling himself for combat. The village wag was now guffawing. Make-good brushed his bug's antennae with a bristle to arouse it. Still it did not move. The young man held his sides. Then Make-good succeeded in provoking the cricket, which exploded in fury and charged headlong. The two creatures tumbled together, striking heavy blows. They shook and strained, the clicks and clacks of battle rising. Presently the smaller one leaped forth, extended its tail, stretched its antennae, and chomped into the enemy's throat. Panicking, the wag pulled the insects apart and stopped the fight. The smaller bug chirped in exultation, as if it had repaid its master's faith in it.

The elated Make-good was admiring his cricket when a rooster came up from behind him, made straight for the victorious insect, and gave it a vicious peck. Make-good shouted with alarm. Luckily the peck had missed its mark, and the bug leaped several feet to safety. But the rooster advanced; already the cricket was under its claw. Pale and frantic, Make-good stamped his feet helplessly. Soon he saw the rooster stretch its neck and shake its head vigorously up and down and from side to side. Looking more closely, he found the insect lodged in the bird's comb and energetically biting it. Overjoyed, Make-good plucked out his cricket and placed it in the cage.

Next day he presented the cricket to the magistrate, who angrily rebuked Make-good for bringing such a puny little bug. Make-good told him what had happened, but the magistrate did not believe it. The magistrate tested the cricket in combat, however, and it defeated all other insects. He matched it against a rooster, with the result that Make-good had described. So Make-good was rewarded, and the insect was presented to the governor. Delighted, the governor offered the insect to the emperor with a detailed account of its prowess.

After the champion cricket had been installed in the royal palace, it was matched against all other fighters of the realm: butterfly crickets, dragonfly crickets, smooth-agile strikes, blue-stripe foreheads, and many other extraordinary specimens. But none could defeat it. Moreover, Make-good's cricket could dance in rhythm to the music of a zither.

The emperor was so pleased that he gave the governor prize horses and silks for clothes. The governor did not forget where the insect had come from, and before long the magistrate received commendation for outstanding service. He too was overjoyed. He excused Make-good from his post as neighborhood head and instructed the educational officer to grant Make-good a degree.

More than a year after these events Make-good's son regained consciousness, his vital spirits restored. "While I was sleeping," he told his father, "I became a cricket. My body felt light. I had the power to make swift leaps, and I grew skilled in combat."

The governor himself richly rewarded Make-good. Within a few years the former neighborhood head acquired one hundred hectares of farmland, a two-story building with ten thousand rafters, and thousands of sheep and oxen. And wherever he went in public, his splendid carriage and finery surpassed those of any nobleman of the age.

—P'u Sung-ling

The Waiting Maid's Parrot

A young waiting maid had been taken into a great household of Szechwan province. She was so beautiful and intelligent that the master favored her over all the other servingwomen and kept her apart from them. It happened that a certain official presented the family with a rare parrot, one so cunning and clever that it could speak with a human voice. The master charged his favorite waiting maid with the care and feeding of the bird as her sole duty.

One day when the maid was feeding it, the bird suddenly spoke: "Take good care of me, sister, and you'll deserve a proper husband for it." Abashed, the maid slapped at the bird with her fan, but it did not flinch. From that time the maid would respond with a jest or a scolding whenever the bird had something to say, until the practice of chattering to it became a habit that she was no longer conscious of. For after all, she was alone in a single room with only a bird in a hanging cage. And if the confidences whispered between them made them intimate companions, whose business was it?

One day the maid was in the bath when the bird had just finished bathing. The creature was so tame that she had not locked its cage, and to her surprise it shook its wings and flew out, circling the room. She snatched at it frantically, but the bird punctured the paper window, looped through it, and was gone, leaving the maid watching helplessly.

Terrified of her master, the girl contrived to hide her guilt. She dressed and moved the cage to the eaves outside her room, then went to him and said tearfully, "Your obedient waiting maid forgot and closed her door to bathe, never expecting to be taken advantage of by someone who came in and released the bird. But I gladly bear the blame and would even die without resentment for my offense."

The master, who knew full well that the other maids were jealous of her, accepted her story. He questioned the rest of the household but could not find the culprit, and the investigation was dropped.

Ten days later the master's wife sent the waiting maid on an errand to a matron named Liang. The matron's unmarried son, Liang Hsü, was spending the day reading in his study. Presently a bird flew in and settled itself on his desk. In a human voice it said, "I have been searching for an ideal mate for you. Why don't you go and have a look?" Startled, Hsü put down his book and chased after the talking parrot. It led him out of his room, and he spied an enchanting maid of sixteen, dressed in dark colors except for a red skirt, shyly enter the house. Now the parrot was nowhere to be seen.

Hsü looked into the girl's face and saw that her beauty was truly exceptional. He found an excuse to follow her into the inner hall, where she conversed softly and fluidly with his mother. There he learned that she was a waiting maid in a mighty household. Yet her demure air utterly captivated him. The waiting maid also noticed the highborn youth and glanced at him from time to time. Though they could not exchange a single word, their affections were engaged.

On returning to her house the waiting maid went to her room, where the empty cage sat beside her bed. Perched on top of it was the bird, peacefully resting with eyes shut and talons curled. As happy as if she had found a royal jewel, the waiting maid snatched at the bird, which fluttered away and protested loudly: "Here I am, sister, nearly spent from dashing about on your behalf, and by good fortune I have found a fine husband for you. Why do you still want to lock me up?" Marveling, the maid listened while the bird told its story.

The bird concluded: "Though I cannot carry you two off beyond the compound wall as the heroic slave of fiction did, I can communicate your heart's desire to him, sister, if he is indeed the man you care for."

The waiting maid blushed but made no reply. "Young people

in love were ever this way," the parrot scoffed. "But someone may be coming, and I must leave now." With that the bird set its feathers in motion and flew off.

The girl had been deeply attracted to Liang Hsü and felt ashamed to be joining the ranks of the master's concubines. Tossing and turning through the night, she was tormented by these two emotions.

The next day when the bird saw that no one was around, it returned to its original perch. The maid beckoned to it and said, "The master dotes on me and will never surrender me to the Liangs. To him that would be 'using a pearl to shoot down a sparrow.' Then again, young Liang is handsome, talented, and rich. Suppose he *were* attracted to a fresh flower; would he stoop to take a waiting maid for his proper wife? I thank you for your trouble, but I fear such an affair must fail. Nothing can be done."

The bird stirred its wings, swept away, and did not come back until evening. Then under cover of darkness it flew into the room

and told the maid, "Young Liang shows his feelings for you in this verse." The parrot recited a poem written by the young man:

> I care not if your fan be plain,
> My love is for your face so fair.
> If we could mount the nuptial bird,
> We'd soar aloft, a wedded pair.

The maid rejoiced to hear this and confided her heartfelt wish to the parrot. As morning approached, she set the bird free.

In his lonely study, Liang Hsü had been thinking of the maid night and day. When he rose that morning and saw a hovering bird, it looked to him like the one that had come before. He joked with it, saying, "My good fellow, can you tell me something of the lady of my heart? Certainly you are a bird among birds; we shall have to have a biography of you so that you will be remembered for all eternity!"

The bird flew down and furled its wings, settling upon a painted screen. It told Liang of the maid's affection and the depth of her anxiety. Elated, Hsü asked if the maid could read. "Somewhat," the bird replied, and then and there Hsü wrote a letter revealing his love and vowing to marry her. He sealed the note and set it on the ground. The parrot swooped down, took the paper in its beak, and flew away, leaving Liang Hsü more astonished than ever by the oddness of it all.

For several days the young man did not see the bird. All news of the maid was abruptly cut off, and he was racked by yearning and despair. Then he heard that a maid in the great household where his beloved served had died and been hastily buried. Suspecting the worst, he made inquiries and verified that it was his own heart's love, though he could not discover the cause of her death. So great was his grief that he almost lost his voice from weeping.

What Liang Hsü did not know was that the maid had seen his note and, ashamed of her inability to write, had removed an earring and given it to the bird to carry back to her intended. The bird was to tell him the location of her parents' home and ask him to visit them and make a gift of money. Her freedom could then be redeemed and she could marry Liang Hsü.

The bird took the earring in its beak and flew aloft, but midway in its course a young tough struck it in the cheek with a rock. The talking parrot tumbled lifeless to the ground.

It was not long before disaster struck the maid also. At first the master had favored her because of her beauty, and everyone had expected that she would take her place among the master's concubines. But she had resisted the idea and had grumbled behind the master's back. When she had put the blame for the lost bird on the other maids and servants, they had looked at her askance even though they had escaped a whipping. They feared that she would cause trouble for them once she became the master's favorite concubine, so they soon attacked her in unison. Having heard her talking to the bird in her room during the night, they spread the slander that she was involved with some man. The tale was quickly sowed in the ear of the master, who began to nurse a deep jealousy. Presently he made a search of the maid's room and came across Liang Hsü's love letter. Enraged now, he had the maid interrogated under torture. Since the story of the parrot partook somewhat of the absurd, the maid herself could not give a clear account of it, and so she was beaten until her body was covered with bruises and her breath scarcely came. Though she was near death, the master did not wait but put her alive into a coffin and ordered her buried in the wilds.

After he learned of her death, Liang Hsü treasured the memory of his buried jewel. He sat, wounded in spirit, and dozed off at his desk. Suddenly a woman entered his dreams. Clothed in feathers, she walked with a dancing gait as she came before him and pulled her lapels together in the ceremonial salute traditionally required of women. "I am the parrot," she said, "and my elder sister, your heart's love, is a parrot as well. Thanks to her virtuous conduct in our previous lifetime, she was transformed into a human, and by chance I was reunited with her. I became concerned that she would be humiliated in an unworthy match, so I respectfully made an occasion to introduce her to you. Who would have thought I would die before accomplishing my mission—leaving my sister's virtue to be defiled, a wrong she bore unto death. The pity of it! And yet something of her vital force still remains, though none save you can help her."

In his dream Liang Hsü was overjoyed and rose to question the vision. Pointing a finger, she said, "One hundred paces beyond the city . . . the tomb of the fair one is not far away . . ." The woman fell to the ground, turned into a crane, and soared to the heavens.

Liang Hsü awoke with a start. At once he ordered his horse and rode out beyond the city wall. He knew of a certain hamlet whose name had the same sound as "hundred paces," the hint in the dream. There he found the burial site, although he did not dare open it right away. He took a room in the hamlet, and when night came he paid his servant to accompany him to the dread place and help him open the tomb. It was not very deep, and when they reached the coffin he thought he could hear the sound of breathing. He broke open the lid, and the maid returned to life.

Delirious with joy, Liang Hsü went to a nearby Buddhist convent and humbly knocked at the gates. He related in full his reasons for coming, and the nuns, who took pleasure in acts of charity, agreed to help him lift the maid from the hole. Liang Hsü carried her to the convent on his own back and left her with the nuns. After seeing to the costs, he went home.

It was over a month before the maid regained her strength. Then Liang Hsü asked a nun from the convent to be his matchmaker and explain as forcefully as possible to his mother that his heart belonged to a girl from a poor home.

Hsü's mother went to see the maid whom she remembered meeting once before, and listened sympathetically to the girl's tearful story. Having always treasured her son, the mother would never thwart his wishes. She took his fiancée home from the convent and severed relations with the maid's former household, so that the girl's whereabouts were kept secret. And Liang Hsü remembered the talking parrot's kindness so well that whenever he met someone who had captured one of these birds, he would buy it and free it.

—Hao Ko Tzu

 Sea Prince

On the Isle of Relics in Shantung multicolored flowers are in bloom the year round. No one has ever lived on the island, and even visitors rarely go there.

A youth named Chang was a lover of things strange and curious. Having heard of the marvelous sights on the island, he prepared wine and food and rowed himself there in a small skiff.

He arrived when the flowers were at their greatest glory, exhaling fragrance that could be scented for a mile. Trees were there too, wide as a dozen spans. He was enraptured and unwilling to leave. He opened his winejar and poured for himself, regretting only that he had no one to keep him company.

Suddenly from among the flowers a beautiful maiden appeared wearing a dazzling red robe. She was unlike anyone he had ever laid eyes upon. She smiled at Chang and said, "I thought I was alone in my enthusiasm for this place, and never imagined I would find a kindred spirit here." Startled, Chang asked her who she was.

"I am a singing girl from Chiaochou," she continued. "I have come with the sea prince, who has taken off in pursuit of scenic wonders. I remained behind because it is difficult for me to walk."

Chang was elated to have so beautiful a maid end his loneliness, and he invited her to sit with him and drink. The maid spoke with a warm and tender turn of phrase that stirred his feelings. Chang was strongly attracted to her, but he feared that the sea prince might come and prevent him from fulfilling his desires.

As he was thinking, a wind sprang up and rustled the trees, which leaned and bent with its force. "The sea prince!" cried the maid. Chang clutched his clothes and looked in astonishment: the maid was gone! Then he saw a giant serpent emerge from the trees, its body thick as a large bamboo. Hoping it would not notice him, Chang hid behind a tree, but it drew closer and began wrapping itself coil by coil around both man and tree. Chang's arms were locked between his legs, and he could not move them. The serpent raised its head and jabbed at Chang's nose with its tongue. Blood poured out of his nose and formed a pool on the ground, and the serpent leaned down to drink it. Chang thought he was going to die.

Suddenly he remembered that he was carrying a bag of fox-bane at his waist. Prying it free with two fingers, he broke open the bag and spilled the poison onto his palm. Then, turning his neck so that he could see his opened palm, he let the blood drip from his nose onto his palm. In moments his hand was full. The serpent drank a little of the poisoned blood, whereupon its body uncoiled, its tail thrashed with a peal like thunder, and it knocked against the tree, cracking the tree in half. Then it lay down on the ground and died, looking like a huge beam.

At first Chang was too faint to get to his feet, but in an hour or two he revived enough to load the serpent on his boat and row home. It was more than a month before he fully recovered from the attack by the beautiful girl who was a serpent spirit.

—*P'u Sung-ling*

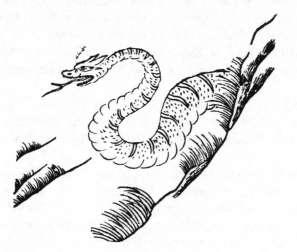

🌸 A Girl in Green

A student called Sung from Yitu, Shantung, was studying in the Temple of Sweet Springs. One night when he was reciting aloud over his open books, a girl appeared outside his window. "How diligently young master studies," she said admiringly. As Sung wondered how such a maiden came to dwell in the mountain depths, she had already come smiling into the room. "Such diligence!" she repeated. Sung rose, surprised. She was graceful and dainty, green-bloused and long-gowned. Though he sensed that she might not be human, Sung questioned her about her home town.

"Can't you see I'm not going to bite you? Why bother with all these questions?" she replied.

Greatly attracted, Sung shared his bed with her that night. When she took off her gossamer jacket, her waist was so slender that two hands could enclose it. Later, as the last night drum sounded, she fluttered away and was gone.

She came every evening after that. Once when they were having wine together, her conversation revealed a knowledge of music. "Your voice is so bewitching," Sung said. "If you would compose a song it would melt my heart."

"For that very reason," replied the maiden," I must not sing." He pleaded, and she explained, "Your serving maid would not begrudge you the song, but what if someone should hear? Still, if you insist, I can only show my poor skills—just a whispered sign of my affection." As she sang, she tapped her tiny foot lightly upon the couch.

No butcherbird must catch
This slave girl's midnight song.
No chill night dew can stay me
From keeping my lord company.

Her voice was a fine hum, the words barely audible. But to the absorbed listener the movement of the melody was lissome and ardent, affecting the heart as it touched the ear.

When the song was over, she opened the door and peered outside. "I must make sure no one is out there." She looked all around Sung's chamber before reentering.

"What makes you so anxious?" he said.

"The proverb 'A ghost that steals into the world fears all men' applies to me." Then she went to bed, but she was still uneasy. "The end of our relationship may be at hand," she said. Sung pressed her for an explanation. "My heart is restless," she told him. "I sense danger. My life will end."

Sung tried to calm her. "Such flutters of the heart are normal," he said. "Do not jump to conclusions." The maiden seemed relieved, and they embraced again.

When the water clock had run dry and it was morning, the maiden put on her clothes and got out of bed. She was about to open the door, but walked back and forth instead. Finally she returned to him. "I don't know why," she said, "but fear is in my heart. Please see me out." The youth arose and escorted her outside. "Keep an eye on me," she said. "You may go back after I get over the wall." Sung agreed. He watched as she rounded the corridor, then could see her no more.

Sung was about to return to bed when he heard her cry out desperately. He rushed toward the sound, but there was no sign of her—only a noise under the eaves. Looking carefully, he saw a spider the size of a pellet with something in its clutches that made a whining sound. Sung broke the web, picked out the object, and removed the threads that bound it. The captive was a green bee on the verge of death. He took it to his room, where it rested on his desk for a long while. When the bee was able to walk, it slowly climbed to the inkwell and pitched itself in. Then it crawled out and walked back and forth until it had formed the word "Thanks." The bee stirred its wings and with a last effort flew out of the window, ending the relationship forever.

—*P'u Sung-ling*

Butterfly Dreams

Chuang Tzu said, "Once upon a time I dreamed myself a butterfly, floating like petals in the air, happy to be doing as I pleased, no longer aware of myself! But soon enough I awoke and then, frantically clutching myself, Chuang Tzu I was! I wonder: Was Chuang Tzu dreaming himself the butterfly, or was the butterfly dreaming itself Chuang Tzu? Of course, if you take Chuang Tzu and the butterfly together, then there's a difference between them. But that difference is only due to their changing material forms."

—Chuang Tzu

🌸 Suited to Be a Fish

Hsüeh Wei was appointed deputy assistant magistrate in Ch'ing-ch'eng county in the year A.D. 759. He was a colleague of the assistant magistrate, Mr. Tsou, and the chief constables, Mr. Lei and Mr. P'ei. In the autumn of that year Hsüeh Wei was ill for seven days. Then he suddenly stopped breathing and did not respond to persistent calling. But the area around his heart was slightly warm, and the family, reluctant to bury him too quickly, stood guard over him and waited.

Twenty days later, Hsüeh Wei gave a long moan and sat up. "How many days was I senseless?" he asked.

"Twenty days."

"Find out for me whether or not the officials Tsou, Lei, and P'ei are now having minced carp for dinner," Hsüeh Wei said. "Tell them I have regained consciousness and that something most strange has happened. Bid them lay down their chopsticks and come to listen."

A servant left to find the officials, who were indeed about to dine on minced carp. He conveyed Hsüeh Wei's request, and they all stopped eating and went to Hsüeh Wei's bedside.

"Did you gentlemen order the revenue officer's servant, Chang Pi, to get a fish?" Hsüeh Wei asked them.

"Yes, we did," they replied.

Hsüeh Wei then turned to Chang Pi and said, "Chao Kan, the fisherman, had hidden a giant carp that he had caught; he offered to fill your order with some small fish instead. But you found the carp in the reeds, picked it up, and brought it back. When you entered the magistrate's office, the revenue officer was sitting east of the gate; one of the sergeants was sitting west of the gate. The revenue officer was in the midst of a game of chess. As you entered the hall, Mr. Tsou and Mr. Lei were gambling. Mr. P'ei was chewing on a peach. When Chang Pi told them how the fisherman had withheld his fine catch, they had him flogged. Then they turned the fish over to the cook, Wang Shih-liang, who was delighted with the carp and killed it. Is not all this true?"

The officials turned and consulted one another and confirmed everything, saying, "But how did you know?"

"Because that carp you had killed was me!" Hsüeh Wei replied to the astounded group.

"Tell the whole story," everyone said.

"When I first took sick," Hsüeh Wei began, "the fever was so intense that I could hardly bear it. All at once I felt stifled and forgot that I was ill. Burning as if I had caught fire, I sought to cool myself. I began to walk with a staff in my hand, unaware that I was dreaming.

"When I had gone past the city wall, an ecstatic mood came to me, as if I were a caged bird or beast gaining its liberty. No one could know how it felt! I made my way into the hills, but I felt more stifled there than before. So I went down to wander by the edge of the river. It was deep and quiet, like a pool. The autumnal quality of the water made my heart ache. Not even a ripple was moving, and the water mirrored remotest space. Suddenly I had a desire to enter the water. I left my suit of clothes on the bank and dove in.

"Ever since my youth I have been fond of the water, but in

adulthood I no longer went swimming. Now I felt eager to enjoy myself so freely and satisfy a long-held desire. But I thought to myself, 'Swimming in the water, man is not as fast as fish are. I wonder if I could enter somehow into the life of a fish and swim rapidly?'

"A fish beside me said, 'There's nothing stopping you if you really want to. We can easily turn you into a regular fish; let me arrange it for you.' And the fish was quickly gone. Shortly a fish-headed man several feet long arrived on the back of a sea monster. Several dozen fish were following him. The fish-headed man read me an edict from the river god:

> Living on dry land and swimming free in the deep are ways apart. Those on land never know the waves unless they love the water.
>
> Hsüeh Wei has expressed a wish to swim and dive, yearning for the leisure of the carefree deep. Finding pleasure in its boundless realm, he would give himself to its pure waters. Tired of high land, he forsakes the mortal world of illusion.
>
> For the present he may become a scaly creature, but this is not a permanent change of identity. Let him be a red carp in the Eastern Pond on a trial basis. But if he should rely on the tall waves to capsize people's boats, the crime he thinks concealed will haunt him; while if he is greedy for bait, blind to the hook on the line, he will suffer in the open.
>
> Do not lose your dignity or shame your fellows. Be diligent in this!

"Hearing the edict, I looked at myself and saw that I was already clad in the scales of a fish. So I flung myself into the water, swimming wherever I wished, atop the waves and down to the deepest deeps, always at ease, gamboling in the three rivers and five lakes of the kingdom. But every evening I had to return to the Eastern Pond, where I was assigned.

"Presently I grew hungry and, finding nothing to eat, began to follow a boat. Suddenly I saw Chao Kan, the fisherman, drop a hook into the water. The bait looked sweet, but I had the sense to be careful. Then somehow it was near my mouth. 'I am a man,' I said to myself, 'who is a fish only for the time being. Can't I make an honest living for myself instead of swallowing his hook?' So I moved away from the boat—but my hunger became worse.

"I thought to myself, 'I am an official who is wearing the suit of a fish merely for fun. Even if I swallow that hook, I can't believe the fisherman would kill me. Surely he would return me to the city.' So I gobbled down the baited hook, and Chao Kan reeled me out of the water. As he reached for me, I cried out over and over, but he would not listen. He ran a string through my cheeks and tied me among some reeds.

"In a short time the servant Chang Pi came and said to Chao Kan, 'Chief Constable P'ei wants to buy a fish, and it has to be a good-sized one.' 'I haven't caught any,' answered Chao Kan, 'but I have over ten pounds of small fish.' 'He ordered me to get a big fish. I have no use for small ones,' said Chang Pi. Then he poked among the reeds and picked me up.

"I said to Chang Pi, 'I am the deputy assistant magistrate of your own county. I shifted into the shape of a fish and have been swimming through the waters of the kingdom. How can you fail to bow to me?' Chang Pi paid no attention, picked me up, and walked on, ignoring even my curses. When we entered the gate to the magistrate's office, I saw the officers sitting down to a game of chess. I shouted at them with all my might, but there was no response at all. They merely smiled and said, 'Quite a catch! Three or four pounds, at least!'

"Then we entered the hall. Tsou and Lei were gambling. P'ei was chewing on a peach. Everyone was delighted with the size of the fish, which was swiftly sent on to the kitchen. When Chang Pi reported that Chao Kan had concealed the carp and tried to fill the order with small fish, P'ei was enraged and had the fisherman beaten. I cried out to all of you that it was your own colleague who had been caught—but far from being set free, I was swiftly put to death. Was that humane? My shouts and tears were ignored as I was handed over to the cook.

"Wang Shih-liang took up his knife and threw me with pleasure onto the chopping block. Again I cried, 'Wang Shih-liang, you are my regular fish-mincer. Would you kill me? Won't you take me to the officials to explain what has happened?' He seemed to be deaf as he pressed my neck against the block and struck off my head. The moment the head fell, I awoke and summoned all of you."

The officials were dumbfounded. Compassion arose in their hearts. But when Chao Kan had caught him, when Chang Pi had picked him up, when the two officers had been playing chess, when the three officials had been in the hall, when the cook had prepared to kill him, the fish was not heard at all even though its mouth was moving.

The three gentlemen threw away the minced fish and from then on never touched that dish. Hsüeh Wei recovered and rose to be assistant magistrate before he finally passed away.

—Li Fu-yen

🌸 Li Ching and the Rain God

When the great military hero Li Ching was still an obscure and humble man, he would hunt with bow and arrow in the Huo mountains, lodging and dining in a local hamlet. The hamlet elder thought him quite remarkable and treated him more and more bountifully as the years went by.

Once Li Ching came upon a herd of deer and pursued them. Dusk was at hand. He wanted to give up the chase, yet excitement carried him forward, and soon in the darkness of the night he lost his way. Where was the road home in this bewildering blackness? Vexed, he pressed on, his anxiety increasing. Then on the horizon he saw the glow of lanterns and headed swiftly toward them.

He arrived at a large mansion with the vermilion gates of wealth and rank. The walls were exceptionally high. After he had knocked for a long time, a servant came out. Li Ching explained that he had lost his way and begged a night's lodging. "It may not be possible to stay overnight," he was told. "The young masters have gone, and only the mistress is at home."

"At least convey my request," Li Ching urged.

The man went inside and then returned. "At first the mistress thought of refusing," he said, "but considering the blackness of the night and the fact that you are lost, she felt obliged to serve as your host."

So Li Ching was invited into the living room. Soon a maid appeared to announce the mistress, who came out wearing a black skirt with a white jacket. She was something over fifty years of age and carried herself with an air of unaffected elegance. To Li Ching it was like entering the home of a leading member of society. He came forward and bowed. Returning his bow, the mistress said, "Since neither of my sons is here, it is not appropriate that you stay. However, the night is dark and the way home uncertain, so that if I refused you, where could I send you? Still, ours is a simple dwelling in the mountain wilds. My sons come and go all the time. Sometimes they arrive in the night and make a lot of noise. I hope you will not be alarmed."

"Not at all," replied Li Ching. The mistress ordered dinner served. The food was fresh and excellent. Strangely for that mountain setting, there was plenty of fish. After dinner the mistress went into another part of the house. Two maids brought bedding and spick-and-span covers which were most luxurious. Then they closed the gate, barred it, and left.

Li Ching wondered what could be coming at night and causing a commotion out here on the wild mountain. He was too frightened to sleep and sat upright, listening. The night was almost half over when urgent knocking sounded at the gate. He heard a servant answer and the caller announce, "The heavens command your son to send down rain in a radius of two miles around this mountain; steady rain until the dawn watch should suffice. Do not delay or cause any harm."

The servant answering the door brought the written order to the mistress inside. "My sons have not come home yet," Li Ching heard her say, "and the order for rain has arrived. We cannot refuse, and if we delay we will be punished. It is already too late to send someone to tell the boys. The servants can't be expected to take it into their own hands. What shall we do?"

"The guest in the living room seems to be a remarkable fellow," one of the young maids said. "Why not ask him?"

Grateful for the suggestion, the mistress knocked at Li Ching's door. "Are you awake, sir?" she asked. "Kindly come out for a moment." Li Ching was swift to comply.

"This is not a human habitation," the lady then told him. "It is the palace of the dragon whose duty is to make rain."

Li Ching was astonished and awed, for the dragon, dwelling in the deep and rising into the clouds, governs the cycle of rainfall over the earth.

"My older son has gone to the East China Sea to attend a wedding," the lady continued. "My younger is escorting his sister for the evening. A moment ago we received Heaven's command to send down rain. There is no time to inform the boys, since thousands of leagues now separate us. A replacement is not easy to find, either. I must venture to trouble you: Would it be possible for you to help us this instant?"

"I am a mortal man, not a rider of the clouds," Li Ching replied. "How would I be able to send the rain? But if there is some art you can teach me, then I am at your disposal."

"Only follow my directions," said the mistress, "and there's nothing you cannot do!" She called for the horse, which was a cream-colored steed draped in black, and directed the servants to tie the rain holder, a little vase, to the front of the saddle. "Don't rein in on the bit," she warned Li Ching. "Follow the horse's own movements. When he stamps his feet and whickers, take one drop of water from the vase and let it fall onto his mane. Be sure not to use more than one drop!"

Li Ching mounted the horse. It vaulted forward, its feet going higher and higher. Li Ching was amazed at its speed and steadiness; he did not realize that he was on top of the clouds. The wind raced by like arrows. Thunder rumbled beneath his feet. Then the horse stamped, and the rider put a drop of water on his mane. Lightning gleamed and clouds parted. Below, he could see the hamlet where he often lodged. 'I've given the hamlet much trouble,' he thought, 'and they have treated me very kindly. How can I repay them? There has been such a long drought that their crops are nearly parched. Now that I have the rain in my hands, why should I be stingy with it?' So Li Ching put twenty drops more onto the horse's mane. Soon the rain stopped, and he rode back to the mansion.

There he found the mistress sobbing in front of the living room. "Oh what a mistake!" she cried. "You promised to use no more than one drop. Why did you use twenty to satisfy your whim? One drop from heaven means a foot of rain on earth. By midnight this hamlet had twenty feet of water! There are no people left. I have been severely blamed and given eighty strokes of the rod. Just look at my back; it's covered with bloody welts. My sons are also incriminated. Oh, what shall I do?"

Li Ching was struck dumb with shame and fear. "Good sir," the lady continued, "you are but a man from the world of mortals, who knows nothing of the movements of cloud and rain. Really, I cannot hold you to blame. But if the dragon king comes looking for you, you will have much to fear. Leave quickly, then, but let me reward you for your pains. Here in the mountains we have little to offer. Perhaps you would accept a gift of two servants—or only one of them, as you choose." And she ordered the two servants to come out.

One came from the east corridor. His face and manner were gentle and pleasing, and he seemed most agreeable. The other came from the west corridor. Hot-tempered and boisterous, he stood restraining his anger.

"We hunters are combative and fierce in what we do," said Li Ching. "Were I to choose the gentle one, wouldn't people take me for a coward? Yet I would not be so bold as to take them both. Since you have offered, I choose the fierce one."

Smiling faintly, the mistress said, "If that is all you wish, sir?" She saluted him and they parted. The servant left with Li Ching, who went a few steps past the gate and looked back. The house was gone. He turned to the servant, but he too had vanished, and Li Ching had to find his way home alone. In the daylight he looked toward the hamlet, and there was water as far as the eye could reach. Only the tips of some trees stood above the flood. No men were to be seen.

It is said that east of the T'ung Pass prime ministers are produced; west of the pass, generals. Li Ching eventually quelled rebellions with his military might, and his victories were unsurpassed. But he never attained the post of prime minister. Can it be because he did not also take the gentle servant from the east corridor?

—Li Fu-yen

 Jade Leaves

In the land of Sung there was a man who fashioned jade into wild mulberry leaves for his lord. The leaves, which took three years to complete, were so perfectly proportioned in stalk and stem, so magnificently realized in the minutest detail, that they could not be told apart when mixed among living leaves. The state supported this craftsman for his skill.

Lieh Tzu objected, "What if heaven and earth needed three years to create a leaf? There wouldn't be many trees. Surely the sage counts on the fruitfulness of nature rather than the ingenuity of man."

—*Lieh Tzu*

⚘ The Wizard's Lesson

Tu Tzu-ch'un lived at the time when the great Sui Dynasty was founded. In his youth he was a devil-may-care sort who never troubled himself to preserve the family's property. With his easy-going, self-indulgent temperament, and his taste for wine and dissolute company, he soon squandered his resources. Friends and relations to whom he turned for help only scorned him for neglecting his responsibilities.

The winter found him in tattered clothes, his stomach empty, barefoot in the streets of the capital, Ch'angan. By day's end he had yet to eat. Confused, with nowhere to go, he drifted toward the west gate of the Eastern quarter. His wretched condition was all too obvious as he raised his eyes to the heavens and groaned.

"Sir, what is it you complain of?" An old man holding a staff stood before him. Tzu-ch'un told his story with indignation over the way his own family had slighted him.

"How many strings of cash would make you comfortable?" asked the old man. In those days, strings of coins were carried in loops of a thousand to each string.

"Thirty to fifty thousand cash would keep me alive," answered Tzu-ch'un, naming a grand sum.

"Hardly enough," said the old man. "Speak again."

"One hundred thousand, then," said Tzu-ch'un.

"Too little."

"One million."

"Still too little."

"Three million!"

"That should do it," said the old man as he drew a single string of cash from his sleeve. "Let this provide for you tonight. Tomorrow noon I shall watch for you at the Persian bazaar. Take care not to be late." And at the appointed time Tzu-ch'un went to the Persian bazaar, where the old man was waiting for him. The man handed Tzu-ch'un three million cash, then left without disclosing his identity.

But wealth rekindled Tzu-ch'un's extravagant desires. Never again, he thought, would he have to live the life of a stranger adrift. He rode the sleekest horses and wore the finest furs and silks. He gathered drinking companions and hired musicians, singing and dancing his way through the pleasure houses of the city. He gave no further thought to managing his money.

In a couple of years Tzu-ch'un had to exchange his fine clothes and costly carriage for cheaper sorts. Then he gave up his remaining horse for a donkey. And soon he gave up the donkey and went about on foot as before. In no time he was back where the old man first found him. At his wits' end, he moaned in anguish by the gates to the quarter. At the sound of his voice the old man reappeared, took Tzu-ch'un by the hand, and said, "I didn't expect to find you like this again. But I shall help you out. How many strings?"

Tzu-ch'un was too mortified to reply. The old man urged him to answer, but the prodigal could only thank him sheepishly for his concern. "Tomorrow noon, come to the place where we met before," said the old man. Tzu-ch'un suppressed his shame and went. He got ten million cash.

Before accepting the money, Tzu-ch'un resolved that he would plan his life and livelihood so sensibly that the famous rich men of history would seem like small-timers. Once he had the money in hand, however, his convictions turned upside down. His self-indulgent nature was as strong as ever, and within a few years he was poorer than ever.

For the third time he met the old man at the familiar place. Tzu-ch'un could not master his embarrassment; covering his face with his hands, he fled. But the old man grabbed the tail of his coat and stopped him. "I should have known you'd need more," he said, giving Tzu-ch'un thirty million cash. "But if this doesn't cure you, there's no remedy."

Tzu-ch'un thought, "When I fell into evil ways and spent everything I had, relatives and friends took no notice of me at all. But this old man has thrice provided for me. How can I be worthy of his kindness?" And he said to the man, "With this sum I can put my affairs in good order, provide the necessities for widows and orphans, and repair my character. I am moved by your profound kindness and will perform any service for you once I have accomplished my tasks."

"Such is my heart's desire," said the old man. "When you are done, meet me on the fifteenth day of the seventh month at the temple of Lao Tzu that stands between the juniper trees."

Since most widows and orphans lived south of the Huai River, Tzu-ch'un transferred his funds to the city of Yangchou. He bought over fifteen hundred acres of choice land there, erected mansions for himself in the city, and set up more than a hundred buildings on the main roads to house the widows and orphans of the region. He arranged marriages for his nieces and nephews, provided all the clan dead with a place in the temple, matched all generosity shown him, and forgave all injuries. When he was done, it was time to seek out the old man.

Tzu-ch'un found him whistling in the shade of the junipers. Together the two ascended the Cloud Pavilion Peak of Hua Mountain at the western end of China. They had gone more than ten miles when they came to a clean, austere residence, unlike any where mortals dwelt, under a canopy of high arched clouds. Phoenix and crane winged through the air. Above them rose the main hall, inside which was an alchemist's furnace nine feet high used for brewing potions and elixirs. Purple flames licking up from it illuminated the door and windows in a fiery light. Around the furnace stood a number of jade-white fairy women, while a black dragon and a white tiger mounted guard front and back.

The sun was beginning to go down. The old man, no longer in mortal garb, appeared now as a Taoist wizard, yellow-hatted and scarlet-mantled. He held a beaker of wine and three white pellets to expand the mind, all of which he gave to Tzu-ch'un. The young man swallowed the pills, and the wizard spread a tiger skin against the western wall and seated Tzu-ch'un facing east.

"Take care not to speak," the wizard cautioned. "Be it revered spirit, vicious ghost, demon of hell, wild beast, hell itself, or even your own closest relatives bound and tormented in a thousand ways—nothing you see is truly real. It is essential that you nei-

ther speak nor make any movement. Remain calm and fearless and you shall come to no harm. Never forget what I have said." With that, the wizard departed.

Tzu-ch'un looked around. He saw nothing but an earthen cistern filled with water. Suddenly flags and banners, shields and spears, a thousand war chariots, and ten thousand horsemen swarmed over hill and dale. The clamor shook heaven and earth. A warrior called the General appeared. He was ten feet tall, and he and his horse wore metal armor that gleamed brilliantly. The General's guard of several hundred men, swords drawn and bows taut, entered the space in front of the main hall.

"What man are you," they cried, "that dares remain in the presence of the General?" Left and right, swords poised, they advanced, demanding Tzu-ch'un's identity. But Tzu-ch'un firmly refused to answer. Infuriated, some wanted to cut him down, others to take a shot at him. Tzu-ch'un made no response, and the General left in a towering rage.

Next came ferocious tigers, poisonous serpents, wildcats, roaring lions, and scorpions, all striving to seize and devour him. Some of the beasts even leaped over him. But Tzu-ch'un remained unmoved in spirit and expression, and in a short time the nightmare melted away.

Suddenly a storm blew up, pelting and soaking, with lightning that made the gloom visible. Reels of fire circled past him left and right. Electric bolts struck before and behind him. Tzu-ch'un could not open his eyes. In moments the waters around the area were ten feet deep, and with the streaming lightning and booming thunder it seemed as if nothing could stop the very rivers and mountains of earth from coming apart. Waves reached his seat, but Tzu-ch'un sat upright and took no notice. Soon everything vanished.

The General returned, this time leading an ox-headed sergeant and his soldiers of hell, together with other weird-faced ghosts. They placed a huge cauldron of boiling water before Tzu-ch'un and closed in on him with spears, swords, and pitchforks. "Identify yourself," they charged, "and we will free you at once. Otherwise beware! We shall pitch you into the cauldron." Tzu-ch'un made no reply.

Thereupon his wife was brought in and thrown onto the stairs before him. "Speak, and we will spare her," they said. They whipped her till her blood flowed freely, some shooting her, some hacking her, some scalding her, some burning her. Unable to bear it, she cried out, "Truly I am but a poor and simple woman, unworthy of a gentleman like yourself. Yet fortune has enabled me to serve you as a wife for over ten years. Now their honors, these ghosts, have taken me, and the pain is more than I can endure. I would never dream of having you crawl on hands and knees to beg for me, but a single word will save my life! Who among men should be considered more heartless if you would deny me that?" She wept, cursed, and scolded, but Tzu-ch'un would not glance at her.

"You think we won't put her to death?" The General said. He ordered a chopping block brought, and they began to cut her up inch by inch, beginning with the feet. She shrieked frantically. But to the end Tzu-ch'un took no notice of her. "This villain is a master of the black arts," said the General, "and must not remain among the living." He ordered his men to cut off Tzu-ch'un's head.

When Tzu-ch'un's head was struck off, his soul was brought before the king of the dead. "Isn't this the heretic of Cloud Pavilion Peak? Throw him in hell!" Tzu-ch'un tasted the torments of hell to the fullest—molten bronze, the iron rod, pounding, grinding, the fire pit, the boiling cauldron, the hill of knives, the forest of swords. But he kept the wizard's words firmly in mind and bore the pain without letting a moan pass his lips. Then the torturers reported to the king that the punishments were completed.

"So devious a villain does not deserve to be reborn a male," decreed the king of the dead. "Let him go back as a female, in the home of Wang Ch'üan, the deputy magistrate in Shanfu county, Sungchou."

After her birth the child suffered many ailments. Hardly a day went by that she was spared acupuncture, cauterization, and harsh medicines. Once she fell into a fire and could get no relief from the pain. Yet not a sound escaped her. She matured into an exceptional beauty, but she never used her voice, and the family regarded her as mute. She never responded to the liberties relatives took with her or the innumerable little insults she suffered.

In the same locality lived an advanced degree holder, one Lu Kuei, who became fascinated by the reports of her beauty and sought her hand through a matchmaker. The offer was declined by the family on account of the woman's muteness, but Lu Kuei argued, "So long as she is worthy as a wife, what need for speech? Rather, she may discourage women who talk too much!" And so the wedding came to be allowed. The young man welcomed his new bride with full ceremony.

For several years the young couple shared a tender, deepening love. They had a son, who showed exceptional intelligence at the age of two. Lu Kuei would cuddle the babe and speak to his wife, though she never replied. He tried many tricks to lure her into speaking, but she remained silent. Then in anger he said to her, "In olden times Lord Chia's wife held him in such contempt that she would not spare him even a smile. However, Lord Chia hu-

mored his wife out of her vow of silence by shooting a pheasant. I am not so ugly as Lord Chia, and I have more culture than skill in archery. Yet you do not speak. If a man's wife scorns him, what use has he for the son?"

Lu Kuei grasped the babe's feet and smashed its head against a rock. The babe's head cracked at once, and blood spurted several paces. Tzu-ch'un felt a sharp pang of love surge in her heart. Her vow of silence slipped from her mind, and a cry of anguish slipped from her lips. And even as the brief cry was escaping her, Tzu-ch'un was sitting where he had been once before. The wizard stood before him. The last watch of night had just begun. Tzu-ch'un saw purple flames coming up from the roof and leaping into the sky. Then the fire closed in on them and burned building and interior.

"Wretched scholar, how you have wronged me!" said the wizard as he lifted Tzu-ch'un by his coiffed hair and threw him into the cistern of water. At once the fires went out and the wizard said, "Your mind had rid itself of joy, anger, sorrow, fear, loathing and desire—all forgotten. Only love remained. Had you not cried out just then, my medicine would have worked and you would have risen beyond your human state to become an immortal. Alas, such men are all too rare. I shall have to make this medicine over again, and you shall have to find your place in the world of men." Then the wizard gestured toward the faraway home. Tzu-ch'un climbed onto the pavilion and looked: the furnace was ruined. Inside was an iron rod as thick as a man's arm. Stripped to the waist, the wizard was hacking it with a knife and demolishing what remained.

After Tzu-ch'un returned home, he was ashamed of forgetting his vow of silence. He took himself to task for his mistake and traveled to the Cloud Pavilion Peak. But he found no human sign and, sighing ruefully, returned home.

—*Li Fu-yen*

The Priest of Hardwork Mountains

Young Wang, seventh son of an established family, lived in town among town comforts. Since childhood he had been fascinated with the occult, and hearing that many immortals could be found on Hardwork Mountains, he traveled there with his book bag on his shoulder.

He made his way to a hilltop where a Taoist temple was secluded. Seated on a mat was a meditating priest. White hair hung down his neck, but he looked brisk and agile in body and mind. Wang paid his respects and spoke with the priest, whose explanation of the powers of the universe seemed wonderfully mysterious. Wang asked to study under him. "I am afraid," the priest replied, "that one who has been so indulged as you may not be able to withstand the hardships." "I'm sure I can," said Wang.

The priest's many disciples gathered as dusk approached. Wang paid his respects to all and remained in the temple. At the crack of dawn the priest summoned Wang, gave him an axe, and told him to join the disciples in searching for firewood. Wang followed his instructions earnestly.

More than a month went by. Wang's hands and feet grew thick with calluses. And as the priest had predicted, he felt that he could not bear the hardships and inwardly resolved to go home.

Returning to the temple one evening, he saw two men having dinner with the master. The sun had already set, but the lamps had not been lit. The master cut a piece of paper into the shape of a round mirror and pasted it on the wall. Presently the moon's light filled the room, and the tiniest thing could be seen.

The disciples scurried to and fro attending to the master's wishes. One guest said, "The pleasure of this wonderful night should be shared by one and all." From the table he took a jar of wine, poured it into the disciples' bowls, and bade them drink their fill. "How can this one jar of wine serve the seven or eight of us?" Wang wondered. But the disciples surged forward again and again to fill their bowls, yet the wine did not diminish.

Soon one of the guest said, "We are honored by this gift of moonlight, but what a shame to drink alone! We should call Ch'ang O, fairy of the moon, to join us." So saying, he tossed a chopstick neatly into the moon, and a beautiful woman materialized out of the moonbeams. Hardly a foot high when she first appeared, she attained human size upon reaching the ground. Her waist was slender, her neck ample. With ethereal grace she performed the Dance of the Rainbow Robe. Then she sang, "Must the Lady of the Moon return to the solitary confinement of her Cold Palace?" Her voice was ringing and resonant, distinct as the flute's tone. When she ended her song she rose in a circling motion and came to rest on the table. Before their startled eyes she turned back into a chopstick.

The three men laughed. One said, "I have never passed a more entertaining evening. But the wine is becoming too much for me. I wonder, could we have our last round in the moon palace itself?" Gradually the three, still seated at the table, entered the moon. The throng of disciples saw them sitting and drinking inside the glowing ball. Even the hairs of their beards and eyebrows could be seen, like reflections in the mirror. In a little while the moon began to dim. When the disciples brought lighted candles, they found the priest seated alone; the guests had vanished. Delicacies remained on the table. The moon on the wall was nothing but a round piece of paper.

"Was there enough to drink?" the priest asked the assembly. "Enough," came the reply. "Then quickly to bed, for you must not miss the morning's firewood gathering," the priest said. Nodding, the disciples retired. Wang was so fascinated by the evening's events that all thoughts of returning home vanished.

After another month, however, he again found the hardships more than he could bear. And the master had not told him how to do a single magic trick! Overcome by impatience, Wang went to the priest and said, "Your humble disciple came hundreds of leagues to receive the teaching of an immortal master. Even if I could not have the secret of eternal life, is there not perhaps some minor teaching you might grant me as a consolation? During the several months I have spent here, I have done nothing but rise early, gather firewood, and return late. At home I never went through such an ordeal."

"I said you couldn't endure it." The priest smiled. "Now I am proved right. Tomorrow evening you shall be sent home."

"Your disciple has labored many days," Wang persisted. "Master, could you not spare me one small trick so that my visit shall not go altogether unrewarded?"

"What technique do you wish to learn?" asked the priest. "I have often observed," said Wang, "that wherever you walk, walls pose no obstacle. I would be happy to learn this one technique."

The master granted the request with a smile. He told Wang the secret and ordered him to recite the spell himself. "Now pass through!" the priest cried. Wang faced the wall but was afraid to enter. "Try to pass through," the priest insisted.

Wang attempted to walk nonchalantly through the wall, but it remained solid and he was blocked. "Lower your head and rush in," said the priest. "Stop shilly-shallying!" Wang stood a step away from the wall. Then he rushed at it headlong—and found it immaterial, as if nothing were there at all. When he turned to look back, he was already past it. Overjoyed, he reentered and thanked the priest.

"Keep yourself pure after you leave; otherwise the technique will not work," the priest warned him. Then he provided Wang with traveling expenses and sent him home.

Once back in town Wang postured like a peacock, preening himself on having hobnobbed with an immortal and boasting that hard walls posed no obstacle to him. His wife would not believe him, however, and Wang decided to amaze her with his trick. He stood a few feet from the wall and then rushed forward—but he bashed his head against the hard surface and fell down. His wife helped him to his feet and jeered when she saw a giant egg swelling on his forehead. Humiliated and indignant, Wang cursed the old priest for having no conscience.

—P'u Sung-ling

White Lotus Magic

This is a story about a man who belonged to the secret Buddhist sect known as the White Lotus. The sect was often at odds with the royal court, and its members were frequently hunted down. The man came from Shansi province, though his name is now forgotten. Probably he was a follower of the rebel leader Hsü Hung-ju, for both men practiced what the court described as "black arts to delude the common folk." Many people became fascinated with his magic and served him as disciples.

One day this magician left the house after placing in his room a basin covered with another basin. He instructed a disciple to keep watch over the basins but not under any circumstances to look inside. The moment his master departed, however, the follower lifted the top basin. He found that the lower one contained water and a tiny reed boat, complete with sail and mast, that floated on the surface. Intrigued, he nudged the boat with his finger, causing it to list. He hastily righted it and put the cover back on.

Presently the master returned. "Why did you disobey me?" he demanded angrily. The follower protested that nothing had happened, but the master said, "My boat has just capsized on the waves. Don't think you can fool me!"

Another evening the master lit a giant candle in his room. Telling his follower to guard the flame carefully and keep the wind from blowing it out, he left and was gone for hours. It was the second watch by the waterclock, and still the master had not returned. Fatigued from guarding the flame, the disciple went to bed for a brief nap. But when he awoke, the candle had gone out. He rushed to relight it.

The master returned shortly and again took the follower to task. "I never fell asleep," the disciple protested. "I don't know how the candle could have gone out." "You made me walk ten leagues in the dark," said the magician angrily.

Some time later the master's favorite concubine fell in love with one of the followers. The master found out but kept it to himself. Then one day he sent that disciple to feed the pigs, and as the young man entered the pen, he turned into a pig on the spot. The master immediately called for a butcher, had the animal slaughtered, and sold the carcass. No one knew anything about it.

The victim's father came to ask after his son, who had not been home in some time. He was told that the disciple must have left, because he had not been seen for a long while. The lad's kinfolk made a wide search but they found nothing at all.

Then another disciple discovered the truth and told the dead man's father. The father reported it to the local magistrate, who decided that a thousand armed men would be needed to make the arrest so that the master could not get away by some trick of magic. The troops surrounded the master's home. With no trouble they took him and his family into custody, placed them in a pen, and began marching with it to the capital.

On the way, when they were crossing the T'aihang Mountains, a giant appeared. He was tall as a tree, with eyes like pots, mouth like a basin, teeth a foot long. The soldiers stood aghast, not daring to proceed. The magician, however, said, "This is a demon that my wife should be able to drive away." The soldiers willingly freed the woman. She shouldered a spear and went up to the giant who swallowed her with one gulp. The soldiers were greatly astonished.

"Since the demon has taken my wife," said the master, "my son will have to do the job." The troops immediately let the son out of the pen, but the demon swallowed him alive as he had the mother. The soldiers gaped at one another; no one knew what to do.

Gnashing his teeth, the master said, "The demon has killed my wife and now my son. It is more than I can bear. I shall have to go myself to take care of it."

Now the soldiers freed the master himself, gave him a weapon, and sent him forth. Full of ire, the giant met him and they tangled. The demon grabbed the master and put him in his mouth, extended his neck, and swallowed the magician down. Perfectly calm and content, the giant then went his way—just like that.

—P'u Sung-ling

🌸 The Peach Thief

Once when I was young, I went to the regional capital during the official examinations. It happened to be the time for the festival to celebrate the beginning of spring. The day before the festival, according to custom, all the merchants and tradesmen paraded to the governor's mansion in a grand show complete with drummers, pipers, and decorated floats.

I went with a friend to watch the parade, which is known as the Presentation of Spring. The masses of tourists and onlookers seemed to form a great wall. Four officials who sat in a hall were dressed in red, the color of celebration, and faced one another east to west. (I was too young then to recognize their ranks.) The hubbub of the crowd and the musicians' din rang in my ears.

From nowhere a man who carried a load on his shoulders approached the hall leading a boy with unbound hair. The man was talking to couriers from the officials. In the clamor of myriad voices I could not hear what he said, though I could make out sounds of laughter from the hall. Soon an attendant dressed in black appeared and loudly ordered a performance. The man climbed the steps of the hall and asked what he should perform. The dignitaries conferred briefly among themselves and spoke to an attendant, who turned to the man and asked what his specialty was.

"We can produce anything out of season!" came the reply. The attendant went to inform the officials, and in a short while came down again to say that the pair should produce a peach.

The man consented, removed his outer clothes, and placed them atop a bamboo box. Then, pretending to talk to the boy who was with him, he said loudly, "Their excellencies don't quite comprehend. How can we procure peaches before the thaw has arrived? But I fear their wrath if we fail. What can we do?"

"Father," the boy replied equally loudly, "you have given your word. There is no way to get out of it."

The performer pondered his problem with an air of dejection. Then he said, "Here's what I think. It is early spring, and the snow is thick. In the world of men there are no peaches to be found. But in the gardens of the Western Queen Mother, the land of perpetual bloom, where the peaches ripen once every three thousand years, nothing fades or falls. So we may find peaches there. We shall have to steal them from the very heavens!"

"How can we climb to heaven?" cried the boy.

"The technique exists," said the father, opening his bamboo box. He took out a coil of rope several hundred feet long, freed one end, and threw it up in the air, where it remained suspended as if hanging from something in the sky. The further he threw it, the further it rose, until it vanished among the clouds. When the

rope was fully played out, the man called to his son, "Come here. I'm old and tired—too heavy and clumsy to go. You'll have to make the climb." Handing the rope to his son, the man said, "If you hold onto this, you can manage it."

The son looked reluctant and complained, "My dear father, this is absurd. Do you expect such a slender line to support me thousands of feet in the air? What will keep my bones together if it should break midway?"

But the father pressed him, "I've already made the mistake of agreeing to fetch the peaches. It's too late for regret. I must trouble you to take the trip. Don't complain, and if we can get away with the fruit, we are sure of a reward of a hundred silver pieces—enough to find you a lovely wife."

And so the boy took the rope and began to squirm up it. As he shifted his hands, his feet followed, the way a spider moves along its web, until he had slowly made his way into the emptiness of cloudy space and could be seen no more.

After a long while, a peach the size of a bowl dropped to earth. Delighted, the performer took it and presented it to the officials. They took their time passing it around for inspection; they seemed uncertain whether it was a real fruit or a fake one.

Suddenly the rope fell to the ground. Alarmed, the performer said, "We're ruined! Someone up there has cut the rope. Where will my son find safety?"

Moments later, something landed on the ground. He looked: it was the boy's head! In tears the man held it up in both hands and cried out, "The theft of the peach must have been discovered by the watchmen! My son is done for!" A moment later a foot dropped from the skies. In another instant the limbs fell down this way and that, until all the pieces were scattered on the ground. In great sorrow the performer picked up each piece and put it into his bamboo box. When he was done he closed the lid.

"I am an old man who had only this one son, and he traveled by my side all my days. Little did I dream, when he took my order, that such a bizarre fate would befall me. Now I must carry him to his resting place." Having spoken thus, the performer ascended the steps of the hall and kneeled. "For the sake of a peach," he said, "I have lost my son. If you would pity this humble soul and contribute something to the funeral expenses, I will be ever vigilant to repay you—even from the beyond."

The awed officials each gave some money, which the performer took and tied to his waist. Then he knocked on the bamboo box and shouted, "You can come out, sonny boy, and thank the donors." A tumbleweed head lifted the cover as a lad emerged and kowtowed to the officials. It was the same boy!

I learned later that the White Lotus Sect could perform this strange trick, and it would not surprise me if the two performers were descended from them.

—P'u Sung-ling

TALES OF
FOLLY AND
GREED

🌳 The Magic
Pear Tree

A farmer came from the country to sell his pears in the market. They were juicy and fragrant, and his sales were booming, when a Taoist priest wearing tattered scarves and coarse cotton clothes appeared at the wagon and begged for some fruit. The farmer shooed him away, but he refused to leave. The farmer's voice rose until he was screaming and cursing.

"Your wagon holds hundreds of pears," said the priest, "and I ask for only one. That's no great loss, sir; why get so angry?"

The crowd tried to persuade the farmer to part with a bruised pear and be rid of the man, but the farmer indignantly refused. At last a market guard saw that the uproar was getting out of hand and put up a few coins for a piece of fruit to throw to the priest.

Hands clasped above his head, the priest thanked the guard. Then he turned to the crowd and said, "We who have left the world find man's greed hard to understand. Let me offer some choice pears to all you good customers."

"Now that you have your pear," someone said, "why don't you eat it yourself?"

"All I needed was a seed for planting," replied the priest. And holding the fruit in both hands, he gobbled it up. Then he took the little shovel that he carried on his back and dug several inches into the ground. He placed the seed in the hole and covered it with earth.

The priest called for hot water, and a bystander with a taste for mischief fetched some from a nearby shop. The priest poured the water over the seed he had planted. Every eye was now on him.

Behold! a tiny shoot appeared. Steadily it increased in size until it became a full-grown tree, with twigs and leaves in unruly profusion. In a flash it burst into bloom and then into fruit. Masses of large, luscious pears filled its branches.

The priest turned to the tree, plucked the pears, and began presenting them to the onlookers. In a short while the fruit was gone. Then with his shovel the priest started to chop the tree. "Teng! Teng!" the blows rang out in the air until finally the tree fell. Taking the upper part of the tree onto his shoulders, the priest departed with a relaxed gait and untroubled air.

During all this the farmer had been part of the crowd, gaping with outstretched neck and forgetting his business. But when the priest departed the farmer noticed that his wagon was empty. And then the suspicion came to him that it was his own pears which had been presented to the crowd. Looking more carefully, he saw that a handle had been chopped off the wagon. In vexation he searched until he found it lying discarded at the foot of a wall. And now he realized that the pear tree he had seen cut down was the handle of his wagon.

Of the priest there was no sign at all, but the marketplace was in an uproar of laughter.

—*P'u Sung-ling*

The Wine Well

The temple named after Lady Wang is in a nook of the Hofu hills, which stand some ten miles to the west of my own county. When she lived is no longer known, but the elders have passed down the following story.

The old woman made her living brewing wine. Once when a Taoist priest stayed at her home, she served him freely—giving him as much to drink as he asked for. Eventually he drank several hundred jars without paying, but the old woman never mentioned it.

Then one day the priest said to the woman, "I have been drinking your wine without having the money to pay you, but allow me, if you would, to dig a well for you." He set to and constructed the well, and a stream of the purest wine gushed forth. "This is to repay you," said the priest. And he went his way.

After that Lady Wang no longer brewed wine; she simply took what flowed from the well to satisfy her customers. And since it was far finer than her previous brews, customers came in droves. Within three years she earned tens of thousands of coppers, and her household became wealthy.

Unexpectedly the Taoist priest returned. The old woman thanked him profoundly. "Was the wine satisfactory?" asked the priest. "Good enough," replied the woman, "but it left no dregs to feed my pigs." The priest smiled and wrote these lines on the wall:

The heavens may be great,
But greater is man's greed.
He made the well, she sold the wine,
But said, "No dregs for feed."

Then he left, and the well ran dry.

—Chiang Ying-k'e

Gold, Gold

Many, many years ago there was a man of the land of Ch'i who had a great passion for gold. One day at the crack of dawn he went to the market—straight to the gold dealers' stalls, where he snatched some gold and ran. The market guards soon caught him. "With so many people around, how did you expect to get away with it?" a guard asked.

"When I took it," he replied, "I saw only the gold, not the people."

—*Lieh Tzu*

Stump Watching

A farmer of Sung saw a rabbit dash into a tree trunk standing in the middle of his field. The rabbit broke its neck and died. From that day, the farmer left his plowing and kept watch by the tree trunk in hopes of getting another rabbit. The farmer never got another rabbit, but he did become the laughingstock of Sung.

—*Han Fei Tzu*

Buying Shoes

There was a man of Cheng who was going to buy himself shoes. First he measured his foot; then he put the measurements away. When he got to the market he discovered that he had left them behind. After he found the shoes he wanted, he went home to fetch the measurements; but the marketplace was closed when he returned, and he never got his shoes. Someone asked him, "Why didn't you use your own foot?" "I trusted the measurements more than my foot," he replied.

—*Han Fei Tzu*

❦ The Missing Axe

A man whose axe was missing suspected his neighbor's son. The boy walked like a thief, looked like a thief, and spoke like a thief. But the man found his axe while he was digging in the valley, and the next time he saw his neighbor's son, the boy walked, looked, and spoke like any other child.

—*Lieh Tzu*

Overdoing It

A man of Ch'u in charge of sacrifices to the gods gave his assistants a goblet of wine. One apprentice said to the others, "This isn't enough for all of us. Let's each draw a snake in the dirt, and the one who finishes first can drink the wine." They agreed and began drawing. The first to finish his snake reached for the goblet and was about to drink. But as he held the wine in his left hand, his right hand kept on drawing. "I can make feet for it," he said. Before he was done, another man finished drawing and snatched the goblet, saying, "No snake has feet." And he drank up the wine.

—*Chan Kuo Ts'e*

The Horsetrader

A horse dealer had an excellent animal for sale, but at the market it attracted no customers. So he went to see the famous horse trainer Po Lo. "In three days no one has noticed my superb horse," he said. "What I'd like you to do is to walk around the horse and inspect it, then walk away—but look back. For this I'll give you a morning's profit from my other sales." Po Lo circled the horse and examined it, walked away, but looked back; and within the day the horse was sold for ten times what it was worth.

—*Chan Kuo Ts'e*

The Silver Swindle

The art of swindling is becoming ever more ingenious. There was an old man of Chinling who took some silver ingots to the money changer's shop at the North Gate Bridge, intending to exchange them for copper coins. He made a point of haggling over the silver content, talking on and on, until a young man came in from outside. The young man's manner was most respectful. He hailed the old man and said, "Your son had some business in Chang-chou that I was involved in. He gave me a letter and some silver ingots to deliver to you. I was on my way to your residence when I happened to see you in here." The young man handed over the silver, saluted the old man, and left.

The old man tore open the letter and said to the money changer, "My eyesight is not good enough to read this letter from my son. Could I trouble you to read it to me?" The money changer complied. The letter dealt with petty family matters and closed with the words, "The accompanying ten taels of fine silver is for your household needs." Looking pleased, the old man said, "Why don't you give me back my silver? Never mind about test-ing the silver content. According to my son's letter, these fine silver ingots he has sent me weigh exactly ten taels, so let's ex-change them for the copper cash."

The shopkeeper put the new silver on the scales and saw that its weight was 11.3 taels. He supposed that the son had been too busy to check the weight when he sent the letter and had written ten taels as an approximation. "The old man can't weigh it him-self," the shopkeeper reasoned. "I may as well let the error stand

and keep the difference." So he gave the old man nine thousand copper cash, the current rate of exchange for ten taels of fine silver.

The old man hauled his coppers away. Soon another customer in the shop began snickering. "It looks like the boss has been cheated. That old man has been a con artist in fake silver for years. I spotted him when he came in, but I was afraid to mention it with him in the shop."

The money changer cut open the silver and found that it was lead inside, which upset him terribly. He thanked the stranger and asked him the old man's address. "He lives about a mile from here," said the customer, "and there's still time to catch up with him. But he's my neighbor, and if he finds out I've given him away, he'll get even somehow. So I'll tell you where to look, but leave me out of it."

Naturally the shopkeeper wanted the man to go with him. "If you'd only take me to the neighborhood and point out his place, you could leave. The old man would never know who told me." The stranger was still reluctant to become involved, but when the shopkeeper offered him three taels of silver, he agreed as if he had no choice.

Together the money changer and the stranger went out of the Han Hsi Gate. Far ahead they could see the old man placing coppers on the counter of a wineshop and drinking with some others. Pointing, the stranger said, "There he is! Grab him quickly; I'm going." The money changer ran into the wineshop, caught hold of the old man, and began to beat him. "You dirty crook! You changed ten taels of silver-coated lead for nine thousand good copper cash."

Everyone gathered around. Unruffled, the old man said, "I exchanged ten taels of silver that my son sent me. There was no lead hidden inside. Since you claim that I used fake silver, show it to me."

The money changer held up the split ingot. The old man smiled. "This isn't mine," he said. "I had only ten taels, so I got nine thousand coppers in exchange. This fake silver seems to weigh more than ten taels; it's not the silver I had to begin with. The money changer has come to swindle *me!*"

The people in the wineshop fetched scales to weigh the silver, which indeed came to 11.3 taels. Turning angry, the crowd ganged up on the money changer and beat him. Thus for a moment's greed he fell into the old man's trap. He went home bruised and burning with resentment.

—Yüan Mei

The Family's Fortune

A tradesman so poor that he barely scraped a living picked up a chicken's egg one day and excitedly told his wife, "Here is the family's fortune!"

"Where?" asked the wife.

"Right here," said the man, showing her the egg, "but it will be ten years before we become rich. I'll take this egg and have the neighbor's setting hen hatch it. Out of that brood I'll bring a female chick home to lay eggs. In one month we can have fifteen chickens. In two years as the chickens give birth to chickens, we can have three hundred. They should fetch ten pieces of silver in the market, and with the money I'll get five calves. In three years when the calves reproduce, I'll have twenty-five. When the calves' offspring give birth in another three years, I'll have one hundred and fifty. This should bring in three hundred pieces of silver. If I use the money to make loans, in three years more I'll have five hundred pieces of silver. Two-thirds of this to buy a house, one-third to buy servants and another wife—and you and I can enjoy our remaining years to the end. Won't that be wonderful?"

All the wife heard was that her husband was thinking of buying another wife. Angrily she flung the egg away, smashing it and crying, "Let's not harbor the seed of disaster!" Enraged, the husband beat her soundly and took her before the magistrate. "This wretched woman," he said "has ruined the family's fortune at a single stroke. She should be executed." The magistrate asked the location of the fortune and the circumstances of the loss. The husband began with the egg and described all that had happened.

The magistrate said, "An evil woman has destroyed a great family fortune in one blow. She deserves to be executed." And he ordered the woman boiled alive.

But the woman protested loudly: "Everything my husband has told you concerns things yet to come. Why should I suffer a boiling for that?"

"The concubine that your husband spoke of buying was also something yet to come," said the magistrate. "Why should you have become so jealous?"

"True enough," said the woman, "but one cannot move too soon in taking precautions against disaster." The magistrate smiled and released her.

Alas! This man schemed from greed, and his wife smashed the egg from jealousy. Both were minds under delusion. The wise man, free of desire, recognizes that even what exists is delusion; how much more so is that which has yet to come!

—*Chiang Ying-k'e*

The Leaf

A poor man of Ch'u read in the book of science and learning known as the *Huai Nan Tzu*: "The mantis preys upon the cicada from behind a leaf that renders him invisible." So he looked in a tree for such a leaf and saw a mantis holding one and waiting for a cicada. The man snatched at the leaf, but it fell to the foot of the tree, where so many other leaves had fallen that he could not find the one he wanted. He swept up several bushels of leaves and returned home with them.

One by one he tried the leaves, asking his wife each time, "Can you see me?" And each time she answered, "Yes." As the day wore on she grew so tired of it that when he held up yet another leaf, she answered falsely, "I can't see you."

The man was struck dumb with delight. He entered the marketplace with the leaf, and holding it in front of him, began grabbing goods in front of the owner's very eyes. The constables tied him up and took him to the judge. The man told the whole story, and the judge burst out laughing and released him.

—*Han-tan Shun*

The Tiger Behind the Fox

A tiger caught a fox. The fox said, "You wouldn't dare eat *me!* The gods in Heaven have made me the leader of all animals. It would be a violation of the gods' mandate for you to make a meal of me. If you doubt it, let me walk in front, and you follow to see if any animal dares stand his ground." The tiger consented and went with the fox, nose to heels. Every animal that saw them fled. Amazed, and agreeing that the fox was leader of all the animals, the tiger went on his way.

—*Chan Kuo Ts'e*

 # Rich Man of Sung

In Sung there was a rich man whose wall was damaged by heavy rain. The man's son said, "There are bound to be thieves if we don't repair it." The father of a neighbor said the same thing. Sure enough, that night before repairs could be made, the rich man lost a lot of his property. The rich man's family praised their son's good sense but suspected the neighbor's father.

—Han Fei Tzu

The Flying Bull

A man who bought a strong, healthy bull dreamed that a pair of wings sprouted from the bull's shoulders and it flew away. He took this for an unlucky sign and feared that he was about to suffer some loss. So he led the bull to the marketplace and sold it for less than he had paid.

Wrapping the money in a scarf, he slung it over his shoulder and set out for home. Halfway there he saw a hawk eating a dead rabbit. He went over and found the bird quite tame, so he tied its leg with one end of the scarf and put it back over his shoulder. The bird thrashed about, and when the man's grip loosened, it soared away with his money.

Forever after, the man told people that there is no way to avoid what fate has arranged.

—P'u Sung-ling

🐑 Social Connections

Old Fei, a farmer, had applied himself to his acres and become tolerably rich. His only regret in life was that he had no friends in high society.

One day during a terrible rainstorm Fei's daughter-in-law was washing vegetables by the riverbank when a small boat anchored beside a willow. Inside there was a scholar sheltering under the dripping mat awning of the boat. His clothes and shoes were drenched; his two attendants were even worse off. The boatman told the daughter-in-law that the passenger's name was Fei and that he held a degree of the second rank. On returning home, she told her father-in-law the surprising fact that the graduate's surname was the same as theirs.

The old farmer gathered up rain gear and hurried to the boat. "What a storm!" he said to the scholar. "Would you care to take refuge in our poor quarters, honorable sir?" Cold and hungry, the scholar gladly accepted. In the farmer's home the required courtesies were performed, and the scholar was delighted to learn that they had the same name. Together they traced the family genealogy, behaving as if they were indeed one happy family.

Old farmer Fei gave orders for a banquet. Holding the scholar by the hand, he led him out under the eaves, remarking, "I can't complain about the way things have gone in the village. Those are my irrigated farms, so many acres; ginger, taro and cane, so many patches; plentiful fishponds; so many banks of wild rice; and besides, there are the mulberry fields and vegetable gardens, and the herb patches that grow in the shade of our mulberries."

Old Fei drew the scholar by the hand to the left side of the hall, where they could see more than ten tall buildings. "My grana-ries," said the farmer. "And those are stalls for the oxen, the sheep, and the hogs. Right and left are the tenant farmers' houses and other bungalows we rent." The scholar nodded continually, his mind dazzled, his eye covetous. When dinner was announced, old Fei invited the scholar to the table.

The viands and delicacies were abundant and clean, far from what one usually finds in a country homestead. The old farmer raised his cup and said, "This brew has been aged five years. We offer it today especially for my honored younger brother." The scholar thanked him profusely, and soon both Feis were warm with spirits. The scholar for his part gave a full account of his pedigree and connections. "This official was my father's class-mate," he said. "And that one my examiner and patron. So-and-so the local official was my examiner, too. Various others are my cousins. At present so-and-so in office in the city are on good terms with me and would satisfy my every wish. Anyone associ-ated with me would be immune from misfortune of any kind."

Old farmer Fei took it in with enthusiasm and reverence. The meal ended, and so did the rains. As the sun was going down, the scholar said goodbye, for he had to leave even though the farmer begged him to stay the night. Sorrowfully old Fei watched him depart.

Next day, wearing his best clothes and taking a multitude of servingmen, the farmer set sail. He reached the city and called on the scholar, who received him cordially. From then on their friendship deepened. Produce from farmer Fei's fields was fre-quently presented to scholar Fei. When the fall harvest was in, part of the new crop was sent to the graduate. At the year's end there would come a gift of preserved meats. The grateful scholar was pained that he could not do something useful in return for the food he had taken. Finally, however, he came up with an idea and consulted a certain police constable with whom he was on close terms. The policeman arranged for a certain bandit to com-mit a crime and frame farmer Fei for it. Soon the farmer found himself in jail.

Seeking help, the farmer's son rushed to the home of the scholar. "Your father has treated me so generously," the scholar said tearfully, "that I would spare nothing to save him. But his offense is not light. This isn't something I can take care of by putting in a word. We're involved with a bunch of real crooks here—what's the best way to deal with this, I wonder?"

The son said, "If there's any way to free my father, we'll follow your instructions to the letter." The scholar told him how much to pay to bribe this official and that official—how much for the magistrate's clerk, the constable, and last of all, the bandit. Paying off the higher-ups and the lower-downs would cost five thousand ounces of silver.

Now, the wealth of a farmer is in his land; there is little cash. Unable to raise the entire amount, the son was forced to give all the deeds for the land and buildings to the scholar, who took possession of the property in the name of other officials. He even circulated petitions and instructions to his superiors and inferiors to milk the son from every possible angle. To meet these demands the farmer's son was reduced to "netting sparrows and unearthing rats," as they say—doing any odd jobs that would turn a penny. At last when the household was stripped clean, the father was set free. One year had gone by.

While in prison, the farmer felt ever grateful to the scholar for keeping him in mind. Old Fei often remarked that he was lucky to know the young man. When he finally returned home and counted up his losses, all that was left to him in the world was his wretched family. The air shook with his great sobs. But before his tears had time to dry, a representative of the receiver of his property arrived.

When the farmer had calmed himself, he fell to wondering why a bandit he had never met could have wreaked such vengeance upon him. So he killed a chicken and took it with some wine back to the jail to feast the bandit and ask the cause of his hatred.

"I ruined you and your family," the bandit said, "yet you have come to feed me. You must be an honorable man. I can no longer conceal the truth, which is that your brother the scholar instructed the constables to do everything." Hearing this, the old farmer realized at last what had happened. He dashed to the graduate's house but time and again was told that scholar Fei was away on business.

Unable to vent his anger there, the old farmer went home and laid the blame on his daughter-in-law. "If it were not for you," he said, "this disaster would never have happened." "Your surnames happened to be the same," she replied, "so I mentioned it to you. I didn't ask you to get involved with the man."

In his anguish the old farmer cursed her, and she was so out-raged that she hanged herself. The son, furious at seeing his wife dead for no reason, also hanged himself. And old Fei, having now neither home nor descendants, put the cord around his own neck too.

—Ching Hsing-shao

𝒮𝒫 A Small Favor

Ting Ch'ien-hsi of Chuch'eng in Shantung was a wealthy and chivalrous man who took pleasure in doing justice and setting wrongs to right. But when the imperial censor in residence ordered his arrest to answer certain charges, Ting disappeared. He traveled to Anch'iu county and there ran into a rainstorm, so he took refuge in an inn. By noon the rain had not stopped.

A young man came with a generous gift of food for Ting. Soon it was dusk, and Ting stayed the night at the young man's home. Both the traveler and his horse were well taken care of. Ting asked the young man his name. "The master of the house is Mr. Yang. I am his wife's nephew," he replied. "He likes to be in the company of friends and has gone out. Only his wife is at home. I fear we are too poor to provide properly for a guest; I hope you will forgive us."

Ting asked Mr. Yang's occupation and learned that he eked out a living by running a gambling den. The next day the rain continued, and Ting and his horse were treated as generously as the day before. At nightfall hay was cut for the horse in bundles that were soaked and uneven. Ting was surprised, and the young man said to him, "To tell you the truth, we are too poor to feed the horse. My uncle's wife just now pulled some thatch off the roof."

Puzzled, Ting thought the lad might be hinting for money and offered him some silver, but it was refused. When Ting insisted, the youth took the silver inside, only to come out again and return it to the guest. "My aunt says that Mr. Yang often goes away for days without any money; he relies on the hospitality of friends. So when a guest comes to *our* house, how can we ask for money?"

Before Ting left he said, "I am Ting from Chuch'eng. When your master returns, please inform him that I would be honored by a visit from him when he is free."

Many years later, there was a famine. The Yangs were in grave trouble and had nowhere to turn. Mrs. Yang casually asked her husband to go and see Ting Ch'ien-hsi, and he agreed. He arrived in Chuch'eng and gave his name at Ting's gate.

At first Ting did not remember him, but when Yang's story was relayed to him he rushed out to greet his guest. Noticing Yang's tattered clothes and worn-out shoes, Ting placed him in a warm room, feasted him, and treated him with love and respect. The next day Ting had a cap and clothes, warm and well-lined, made for the guest. Although Yang was overwhelmed by Ting's hospitality, his worries were increasing, for he was anxious to get relief for his family. Several days went by, however, and his host still made no mention of sending him home with parting gifts.

At last Yang said apprehensively to Ting, "There's something I cannot keep from you. When I left home, we didn't have even a peck of rice. Now I have already received so much of your generosity, and while I am surely delighted, what of my family?"

"Nothing to worry about," replied Ting. "I've already taken care of them for you. Please don't let it concern you. Stay with us a little longer, and then I'll help you with your travel expenses." Ting summoned a group of gamblers and arranged for Yang to take a commission out of their game. During the night Yang made one hundred pieces of silver.

After this Ting sent him home, where Yang found his wife in new clothes, with a young maidservant attending her. Amazed, he asked what had happened. "The day after you left," she said, "carts and men on foot came with gifts of cloth and silk and beans and grain, enough to fill the whole house! They said it was a present from Mr. Ting. He also sent a serving maid to do my bidding."

Yang's gratitude knew no measure. From then on he became prosperous and did not have to follow in his former occupation.

The Recorder of Things Strange says: To enjoy company and entertain guests is what drinkers, gamblers, and floating types are best at. More remarkable is Yang's wife, who offered such generous hospitality though she was no drinker or gambler herself. What humanity is there in those who accept a favor but do not reciprocate? Ting is a man who did not forget even the gift of one meal.

—*P'u Sung-ling*

🌰 Pitted Loquats

Chu I-chün, a member of the Imperial Academy, was on friendly terms with a Taoist priest. In the temple were two loquat trees, and every year when the fruit ripened, the priest would offer some to Chu. The loquats never had pits, and when Chu asked why, the priest replied that they were a supernatural species. Chu received this explanation with skepticism.

The priest loved fine food and particularly relished steamed pork. One day Chu invited him for dinner, and instructed his servant to purchase a pig and carry it through the house in the priest's presence. In a short while the meat was presented at the table, well cooked and succulent. They ate their fill, and when the feast ended, the priest asked Chu how the meal had been prepared so quickly.

"It's really a simple trick," said Mr. Chu. "I'll tell you if you tell me the secret of your loquats."

"Nothing to it, really," said the priest. "When they first flower, I pinch out the fine hair from the core."

"Well then," said Chu, "as for the meal, I had it cooked yesterday." And smiling broadly, heads thrown back, they parted.

—*Tai Yen-nien*

 Memory Trouble

In the land of Ch'i in eastern China there was a man who had so much trouble remembering things that he would even forget to stop when he was walking or to get up when he was sleeping. His wife grew worried and said, "They claim that Ai Tzu has skill and knowledge to cure the most deep-seated ailments. Why don't you go and put yourself under his care?"

The man agreed. He mounted his horse, took bow and arrows to defend himself on the way, and set off. But soon he felt pressure in his bowels and got off his horse to relieve himself by the side of the road. The arrows he planted in the ground, the horse he tied to a tree.

When the man was finished, he looked to his left and spotted the arrows. "That was close!" he said. "Where did those stray arrows come from? One of them could have hit me!" He looked to his right and saw the horse. "That was some scare," he thought, "but I have gained a horse." When he took the reins, he stepped into his own dung. Stamping his foot, he said, "I've walked into some dog dung and dirtied my shoes. What a shame!"

He turned the horse toward the way they had come and laid on the whip. Soon he was back at his house. He paced to and fro before the main gate. "Who could live here?" he asked himself. "Don't tell me it's Ai Tzu's place!" His wife saw him and realized that his memory had failed again. She scolded him, but the man said forlornly, "My good woman, I don't believe we are acquainted. Why should you speak so harshly to me?"

—Lo Cho

🌸 Medical Techniques

Chang was a poor man of Yi county in Shantung. He happened to meet a Taoist priest on the road who was skilled in physiognomy. The priest read his features and said, "You ought to make your fortune in some profession." "What should I pursue?" asked Chang. The priest eyed him again. "Medicine should do," he said.

"How could I go into that," replied Chang, "when I can hardly read?"

The priest smiled. "A famous doctor doesn't have to read much. Do it, that's all."

Chang returned home and, since he had no work anyhow, resolved to follow the priest's advice. He got together some quack remedies and cleared a place to set up shop in town. There he displayed fishes' teeth, honeycombs, and other such, hoping to scare up a few cups of rice with his slippery tongue. But day after day no one took any notice of him.

It happened that the governor of Ch'ingchou was troubled by a cough and ordered his subordinates to summon medical advice. Since Yi county was far off in the mountains, doctors were scarce. But the county magistrate, fearful lest he fail in his duty, ordered the chiefs of the hamlets to produce one. By consensus they recommended Chang.

The county magistrate summoned Chang to come at once. But Chang himself suffered from an asthmatic cough which he could not relieve, so the official command frightened him and he firmly declined. The magistrate would not accept his answer and ordered Chang delivered under escort to the governor.

Chang's carriage passed through remote mountains, where water was precious as nectar. His great thirst made his cough worse, and he stopped at a hamlet to find water. No one could spare any, though he begged everywhere. Then he spotted a woman straining a mess of wild vegetables in a small amount of water. Some liquid, turgid as phlegm, remained in the pan, and the parched Chang asked for it. The woman gave it to him, and a short while after he drank it his thirst eased and his cough vanished. "An effective remedy, it seems," he thought to himself.

When Chang reached the governor's headquarters, physicians from the various counties had already tried out their treatments with no success. Chang asked for a secluded spot, where he pretended to prepare a prescription. He passed the medicine around for people to see. At the same time, he sent someone to find pigweed and bishopweed among the common folk. Then he strained them and presented the juice to the governor, whose cough improved after a single dose. Overjoyed, the governor rewarded Chang richly and gave him a gold plaque to display. And in this manner Chang's name was made. His doorway became as crowded as the marketplace, and all who came were cured.

Once a man came to him with a case of typhoid, but Chang

was drunk and dosed the patient with the medicine for malaria. When Chang awoke, he realized his mistake but was afraid to tell anyone. Three days later a grand ceremonial procession arrived at his gate to thank him, for the typhoid victim had recovered after a spell of severe vomiting and diarrhea. Incidents of this kind occurred frequently.

From then on Chang became a wealthy man without holding office, and the value of his services continued to rise with his rising reputation. He would visit only those who offered him large fees and comfortable transportation.

Another famous physician was Old Man Han, who lived in Yitu of Ch'ing province. Before he became famous he peddled tonics in the four corners of the realm. One night when he was far from any inn, he was given lodging by a family. It happened that their son was dying of typhoid, and the parents begged Han to treat the boy. Han feared that if he refused, they would throw him out; yet the truth was that he had no cure for the disease. Pacing back and forth wondering what to do, he rubbed his hand along his body, and some grime came off in his fingers. In his distraction he kneaded the dirt into a pellet. Then the thought struck him that he could dose the boy with it, for it certainly could do no harm. If there was no improvement by dawn, Han would have already earned a meal and his night's rest.

Han gave the boy the pellet, and in the middle of the night the boy's father came knocking furiously at Han's door. Sure that the boy had died, the physician leaped out of bed and vaulted the compound wall to avoid a beating. The father pursued the fleeing doctor for over a mile and finally caught up with him. Then Han learned that the patient had sweated and recovered. They led the medical man back to a sumptuous banquet and sent him on his way richly rewarded.

—P'u Sung-ling

❧ The Lost Horse

A man who lived on the northern frontier of China was skilled in interpreting events. One day for no reason, his horse ran away to the nomads across the border. Everyone tried to console him, but his father said, "What makes you so sure this isn't a blessing?" Some months later his horse returned, bringing a splendid nomad stallion. Everyone congratulated him, but his father said, "What makes you so sure this isn't a disaster?" Their household was richer by a fine horse, which the son loved to ride. One day he fell and broke his hip. Everyone tried to console him, but his father said, "What makes you so sure this isn't a blessing?"

A year later the nomads came in force across the border, and every able-bodied man took his bow and went into battle. The Chinese frontiersmen lost nine of every ten men. Only because the son was lame did father and son survive to take care of each other. Truly, blessing turns to disaster, and disaster to blessing: the changes have no end, nor can the mystery be fathomed.

—*Liu An*

☙ The Deer in the Dream

A woodsman of the state of Cheng was gathering firewood in the forest when he met a frightened deer. He stood before the animal and struck it dead. Afraid someone else would find and appropriate it, he hastily hid the deer in a ditch and covered it with the wood he had gathered. Presently, however, the place where he had hidden the deer slipped his mind, and he ended up thinking it had all been a dream.

As the woodsman continued on his way, he sang a song about what had happened. A passerby on the road overheard the song, and making use of the words, found the deer and took it home. The passerby told his wife, "I heard a woodsman who dreamed he had a deer but didn't know where it was. I now have it, so plainly his dream was true."

"Might it not be," said his wife, "that *you* dreamed a woodsman had a deer? Why must there be a woodsman at all? Since you now have the deer, doesn't it mean that *your* dream is true?"

"Well, since the deer is in my possession," said the man, "what difference does it make whether he was dreaming or I was?"

When the woodsman who had killed the deer returned home, he was distressed over losing the animal. That night he dreamed of the place where he had hidden it and also of the passerby who had taken it. Early next morning he searched and found the man just where the dream had indicated. He took the man to court over the deer, and the case came before the magistrate.

Addressing the woodsman, the magistrate said, "At first when you really got a deer, you called it a dream. And when you really dreamed of getting a deer, you called it real. The passerby really got your deer, and you are challenging him for it. His wife says that you are claiming another's deer from a dream, and that no one got your deer. Now then, the passerby and his wife have possession of this deer, but I advise that it be divided between you."

The magistrate brought the case to the attention of the king of Cheng. "Ah well," said the king, "I suppose you will in turn be dreaming that you divided the deer?" The king consulted the prime minister, his chief adviser, who said, "I cannot tell dreaming from waking. Only the Yellow God-king or Confucius could do that. Since we have neither, it seems best to accept the magistrate's decision."

—*Lieh Tzu*

✺ Loss of Memory

Hua Tzu of the state of Sung suffered a loss of memory in his middle years. Whatever he took in the morning was forgotten by evening. Whatever he gave in the evening was forgotten by morning. On the road he would forget to move ahead. Indoors he would forget to sit down. Here and now, he has forgotten then; later he will not remember the here and now.

His whole household was plunged into confusion by his ailment. Finally he sought the help of an astrologer, but divination provided no answer. He sought the help of a medium, but prayer could not control the problem. He visited a physician, but the treatment brought no relief.

In the state of Lu there was a Confucian scholar who claimed that he could cure the disease, and Hua Tzu's wife paid him half their estate to do it. "No sign or omen," said the Confucian, "can solve this. No prayer can preserve him. No medicine will work. I must try to transform his mind and alter his thinking; then there may be hope." The scholar stripped Hua Tzu, and the naked man demanded clothes. The scholar starved Hua Tzu, and he demanded food. He locked Hua Tzu in a dark room, and he demanded light.

The delighted Confucian said to Hua Tzu's son, "This illness can be cured. But my remedy is a secret handed down for generations, a secret that has never been revealed to anyone outside our family. I must ask you to dismiss all your father's attendants so that he can live alone with me for seven days." The son agreed.

No one knows what methods the scholar used, but Hua Tzu's ailment of many years cleared up. When Hua Tzu realized that he was cured, he went into a tremendous rage. He chastised his wife, punished his son, and drove off the Confucian with weapons. People seized Hua Tzu and asked him why he did this.

"In my forgetfulness I was a free man, unaware if heaven and earth existed or not," said Hua Tzu. "But now I remember all that has passed, all that remains or has perished, all that was gained or lost, all that brought sorrow or joy, all that was loved or hated— the ten thousand vexations of my decades of life. And I fear that these same things will disturb my mind no less in times to come. Where shall I find another moment's oblivion?"

—Lieh Tzu

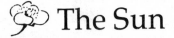 # The Sun

During his travels to the east, Confucius came upon two boys arguing. He asked them why, and one replied, "I say that the sun is closest to us when it first comes up, and farthest away at noon."

"No," said the other, "it's farthest from us when it rises and closest at noon."

The first boy said, "When the sun rises, it's as big as a chariot's canopy. At noon it's the size of a plate. Isn't this because the farther is smaller, the closer is larger?"

The second boy said, "When the sun rises it's still cool, but by noon it's quite hot. Isn't this because what's closer is hotter, and what's farther is cooler?"

When Confucius could not solve the problem, the two boys said, "Who says you know so much?"

—*Lieh Tzu*

THE ANIMAL
KINGDOM

A Faithful Mouse

Yang T'ing-yi tells about the time he saw two mice come into the open and a snake gobble one of them down. The other mouse, eyes popping like peppercorns, kept his distance as he glared. The snake got the mouse it had caught into its belly and slithered for its hole. It was more than halfway in when the second mouse dashed forward and clamped his teeth around the snake's tail. Furious, the snake backed out. The ever-nimble mouse darted to safety in a flash. The snake gave chase but failed to catch the mouse, so it returned to its hole. As it was entering, the mouse seized its tail exactly as he had before. Each time the snake crawled in, the mouse struck; each time the snake came out, the mouse ran. This went on for quite a while, until the snake spat the dead mouse onto the ground. The second mouse came up and cried over his friend. Then, squeaking dolefully, he picked up the corpse in his mouth and left. My friend Chang Li-yu wrote a poem in its honor called "The Faithful Mouse."

—*P'u Sung-ling*

🌹 The Loyal Dog

A man of Luan had run afoul of the law and was about to be executed. His son scraped together all the family's savings, which came to a hundred pieces of silver, to appeal the case to the governor. When the son mounted his donkey and set out for the capital, his black dog followed after him. The son shouted at the dog to go home, but the moment he started to ride away, the animal followed again. Even when he whipped the dog it hung around and sidled after him.

Man, donkey, and dog had gone a dozen miles or so in this manner when the son dismounted and hurried to the side of the road to relieve himself. Then he began throwing stones at the dog, until the animal finally fled for its life. Once free, the man and the donkey set out and made good time, when suddenly the dog reappeared. Breathing so hard its sides were like pumping bellows, it snapped at the donkey's tail and ankles. Angrily the son laid his whip to his pet. It yelped and barked, but leaped ahead and snapped at the donkey's head as if it were trying to block the way.

Angrier than ever, the son turned the donkey around and rode back the way he had come, driving the dog before him. When he had it running a long way ahead of him, he swung around and galloped toward the capital.

It was nightfall when he arrived. He felt for the satchel of silver at his side. Half the money was missing! He broke into a heavy sweat and lost his wits completely. All night he tossed and turned, until it struck him that there must have been a reason for the commotion the dog had made.

He had to wait until early morning for the city gates to open. Then he rode carefully back the way he had come, with a sharp eye out for his money. Travelers on the roads were thick as ants, however, and he figured there was little chance of finding it. He came to the spot where he had dismounted to relieve himself. There in the high grass he saw the dog's lifeless body, its fur soaked as if it had been bathed. He lifted the dog's ear and saw the silver, intact, before his very eyes.

Moved by the dog's devotion, the son bought a coffin and buried it. The place is still known as the Loyal Dog's Tomb.

—*P'u Sung-ling*

Black and White

The philosopher Yang Chu had a younger brother named Pu. One day Pu left the house wearing white clothes. A storm came up and soaked them, so he changed into some dark ones. When he returned home, his dog did not recognize him and barked furiously. Pu was angry and raised his arm to beat the dog, when his older brother said, "Don't hit him. Would you recognize your dog if he went off white and came home black?"

—Lieh Tzu

ᘒ The Dog
Goes to Court

In the fall of the year a traveler was riding home from a business trip with five or six hundred pieces of silver. In a county called Chungmou he dismounted from his mule and sat by the roadside to rest. A young man with a long pole on which he was carrying a dog sat down beside him.

The dog whimpered piteously at the merchant as if begging for his freedom, so the traveler bought the dog from the youth and set it loose. Meanwhile the young man noticed that the merchant's sack was heavily loaded. He quietly followed the traveler to a deserted spot, where he beat him to death with the pole. He dragged the body to a small bridge that crossed a stream, covered the corpse with sand and reeds, shouldered the sack, and left.

Seeing the stranger dead, the dog kept out of sight but trailed the youth home. He took note of the place and left, running all the way to the county courthouse. It happened that the judge was opening the day's sessions, and the sergeants-at-arms were in position, strict and severe. The dog dashed forward and made a great outcry, half moaning, half appealing. He could not be driven off.

"What's your complaint?" asked the judge. "I'll send an officer to follow you." The dog led the officer to the foot of the bridge where the traveler's body was hidden; then he barked toward the water. The officer pulled up the reeds and discovered the corpse. He reported back to the judge, but there was no way to apprehend the culprit. The dog also returned to the courthouse, where he barked and flung himself about. "You know who did it?" asked the judge. "I might as well send officers to follow you."

This time the judge dispatched several men with the dog. They trailed him for seven or eight miles until they came to a house in a remote village. The dog entered it, leaped on a young man inside, and savaged him, tearing his clothes and drawing blood. The officers dragged the man to the courthouse, where he confessed and gave details of his crime. "The merchant's silver has not been touched," he told them, and they returned to the house for it. Inside the merchant's sack of money they also found a document with his name and village.

The judge passed sentence on the young man and had the sack placed in the public treasury. Again the dog planted himself and barked without letup. The judge reflected, "Although the merchant is dead, his family must be alive. The sack belongs to them; that must be why the dog is barking." So he sent his officers off to the dead man's village. The dog followed.

When they arrived, the merchant's family was terribly shocked to learn that he was dead. The man's son went back with the officers to Chungmou, where the culprit had already died in jail. The judge took the sack of silver, checked it carefully, and turned it over to the son.

The dog meanwhile followed the son to Chungmou and then back again when the coffin was escorted home. And in all the hundreds of miles that they covered, the animal conducted itself like a human being.

—Hsü Fang

🐾 The Tale of
the Trusty Tiger

One morning a woodsman was walking through a bamboo grove.
All of a sudden he lost his footing and fell into a tiger's lair. Two
little cubs were inside the pit, which was shaped like an upside-
down bowl. Sharp, jagged stones stuck out on three sides. The
front wall was smooth but well over ten feet high. It was an
unbroken drop like a slide—the tiger's pathway.

The woodsman leaped up and fell back down a number of
times. Then he walked around inside at his wit's end. Tearful, he
awaited his death. The sun set, and the wind brought the tiger's
howl. She scaled the wall and entered the pit with a freshly killed
elk, which she tore in half for her two cubs. Next she saw the
woodsman cowering on the ground. She spread her claws and
flexed her front legs, but then circled him pensively as if she had
had a second thought. Instead of attacking, she fed him a scrap of
the meat. As he ate it, she went into her niche with her cubs to
rest.

The woodsman figured that the tiger was not hungry now but
would surely devour him come morning. Instead, the tiger leaped
out of the pit at the crack of dawn. At midday she returned,
bringing a musk deer, which she fed to her cubs. And as before,
she threw the leftovers to the famished woodsman, who devoured them. To relieve his thirst he drank his own urine. This
went on for nearly a month, and gradually he became used to the
tiger.

One day when the cubs had grown husky, the tiger put them

on her back and went out. Frantic, the woodsman howled to the heavens, "Save me, Your Majesty!" Within moments the tiger came back, folded her forelegs, and lowered her head before the woodsman. He climbed onto her back, and she vaulted the wall. There on the surface she set the woodsman down, took her cubs, and went on. He was left alone by a dark cliff in dense grasses, where there was no song of birds or any noise but the shrill wind blowing out of the dark wood. More frantic than ever, the woodsman called out, "Your Majesty!"

The tiger turned and regarded him. Kneeling, the woodsman pleaded, "It was Your Majesty's kindness that kept me alive. But now we shall be lost to one another, for I fear I shall not escape wild beasts. To guarantee my safety, could you favor me with your escort to a main highway? I shall be in your debt to my dying day."

The tiger nodded and preceded the woodsman to the main road. Then she turned around and stood staring at him. Again the woodsman expressed his thanks: "I'm a poor man of the west gate, and after I leave you, we're not likely to meet again. But when I get home I'm going to raise a pig, and I will wait for you with the pig on a certain day at a certain time by the post station. Come and enjoy a feast. Don't forget."

The tiger nodded. The woodsman wept, and the tiger wept too. When the woodsman arrived home, his astonished family questioned him, and after he had told his story they rejoiced together. At the appointed time he prepared a pig and took great pains in butchering it. The tiger, however, arrived at the appointed place before the appointed hour. Unable to find the woodsman, she actually entered the west gate, where she was seen by the residents. They summoned some hunters, who closed the main gate and wings and gathered around the tiger, their spears at the ready, arrows to the bow. They agreed to capture her alive and present her to the local authorities.

The woodsman ran to the rescue, crying out to the crowd, "This tiger once kept me alive. I beg you all not to harm her!" But the hunters caught the tiger and took her to the government office. The woodsman went along, beating a drum and shouting. Angered, the officials questioned him, and he told them the whole story. They did not believe him.

"Let me prove it, then," said the woodsman, "and I'll suffer a beating if what I say is false."

The woodsman put his arms around the tiger and said tearfully, "Your Majesty saved my life?" The tiger nodded. "Your Majesty entered the gate to keep our appointment?" The tiger nodded again. "I shall plead for your life; if I fail, I shall die with you." As the woodsman spoke, the tiger's tears fell to the ground. Of the many thousands who witnessed this, not one stood unmoved. The astounded officials hastened to free the tiger, then led her to the post station and threw her the promised pig. The tiger straightened her tail and made a feast of the pig. Afterwards she looked once at the woodsman and departed. Later this district was named after the trusty tiger.

—Wang Yu-ting

✑ The Repentant Tiger of Chaoch'eng

A woman of Chaoch'eng who was over seventy years old had an only son. One day he went into the mountains and was eaten by a tiger. The old woman grieved and grieved, ready to give up her life. Then with vociferous cries she complained to the local authorities.

"How can a tiger be subject to the law?" said the magistrate with a smile. This only aggravated the old woman's tantrum, and when the magistrate scolded her she would not be intimidated. Because he felt sorry for her, he kept his own temper and even ended by agreeing to have the beast apprehended.

The old woman knelt down before him. She refused to leave until the warrant was actually issued, so the magistrate called for a volunteer on his staff to go and make the arrest. Li Neng, an agent who was drunk at the time, came forward and took the warrant, and the old woman left satisfied.

When Li Neng sobered up, he regretted his offer. Still, he assumed that the warrant was only a ruse to stop the old woman from creating a nuisance, so he turned it back in to the magistrate casually. But that official said angrily, "You gave your word you'd do it. How can I accept a change of mind?"

Cornered, the agent appealed for another warrant to deputize some hunters, and this the magistrate granted. Day and night Li Neng and his hunters now stalked the mountain hollows in hopes of catching a tiger. But more than a month passed without success, and the agent was given a severe beating of one hundred strokes. Having nowhere to turn for redress, he presented himself at the shrine east of the town. There he called on his knees for the local deity, crying until he had no voice.

Soon a tiger came up. Li Neng was aghast, expecting to be eaten. But the tiger entered the shrine and, looking steadily at the agent, sat down on its haunches in the doorway. Li Neng called to the tiger as though it were a deity: "If it was you who killed the woman's son, then you should submit to my arrest." Then the agent took out a rope and tied it around the tiger's neck. The tiger dropped his ears and accepted the rope, and the agent led the beast to the magistrate's office. The magistrate asked the tiger, "That woman's son—you ate him?" The tiger nodded.

"Those who take life must die," continued the magistrate. "That law stands from oldest times. Besides, the poor woman had only one son. How do you suppose she'll survive the years that remain to her? However, if you should be able to serve as her son, I shall spare you." Again the tiger nodded. So they removed the ropes and sent the animal away, though the old woman was grieved that the magistrate did not make the tiger pay with its life.

When the morrow dawned, the old woman opened her gate to find a deer's carcass, which she took and sold for her daily necessities. This became a custom, though sometimes the tiger would bring money or silk in his mouth and flip it into her yard. And so the woman became quite well-to-do—far better cared for than when her son was alive. She grew to feel deeply grateful for the tiger's kindness. Eventually the tiger would come and lie under the eaves of her house the whole day, and the people and livestock no longer feared it.

After several years the old woman died, whereupon the tiger came and bellowed in the front hall. The woman had saved up enough for an ample burial service, and her kinsmen laid her to rest. When the mound over the tomb was completed, the tiger suddenly bounded up. The mourners fled, and the tiger went straight to the front of the tomb, roared thunderously for a long while, and then departed. Local people set up a shrine to the loyal tiger by the eastern outskirts of the township, where it remains to this day.

—*P'u Sung-ling*

Tiger Boys

In recent years my village has had a number of tigers, and they have chewed up more people than you can count. Travelers through most of China, in fact, have been similarly plagued. Some say tigers are agents of the Highest in Heaven, helping chase down those who have escaped their appointed death by violence. Others say tigers are manifestations of fierce demons and vengeful spirits in a state of agitation and frustration. There may be some truth in both views, but nothing is quite so remarkable as the story about Old Man Huang.

Old Huang was from Mihsi, several miles from the town of Chiao. He had three fully grown sons. In the spring of the year, he sent them to plow his fields in the hills, and for several days they went out at sunup and returned home at dusk. One evening a neighbor said to him, "Your fields are overgrown with weeds."

"How could that be?" replied Old Huang. "My boys plow it every day."

"I'm afraid not," answered the neighbor. Puzzled, the old man secretly followed his three sons when they went out next morning. He saw them enter the woods in the hills, remove their clothes, and hang them on a tree. Then they changed into tigers. Roaring and leaping, they emerged from the woods.

Old Huang was terrified. He ran home and confided what he had seen to his neighbor, then bolted his door and hid. The three came home that night and called at the gate for a long time, but no one answered. At last the neighbor came out and explained that their father would no longer know them as sons because of what he had seen in the hills.

"It's true," admitted the boys. "But we are not acting of our own free will. The Highest in Heaven compels us." Then they cried to their father, "How could we fail to repay your boundless generosity? We feel helpless because you have long been destined for calamity. These past few days we have been ranging the hills in hopes of finding someone who could take your place. And even now, after you've discovered us, we can't disobey our orders. In the collar of my clothes is a small booklet. Kindly get it for me, Father, otherwise you're surely done for, and we three will be responsible for your death."

Old Huang took a lantern and searched in the collar, where he found the little booklet. It was filled with the names of those in Chiao who were to be killed by tigers. His own name was second from the top. "What can be done?" the old man asked.

"Just open the gate," said the boys. "We've thought of something." Old Huang did so. The boys took the booklet and, weeping, bowed to him. Then they said, "This is all according to the decree of the Highest in Heaven. Now put on several layers of clothes, but don't fasten the belt. Stick yellow paper on top, and pray fervently on your knees. We have our own way of rescuing you."

Old Huang did as he was told. His three sons leaped over him from behind, each tiger catching a layer of clothes in its mouth. Then they dashed off with a great roar and never returned, and the old man is alive to this day.

From ancient times there have been many cases of men turning into tigers. Without fail, their hides and their faces were transformed. But it is unheard-of for tigers to remain among men as these three boys did. Moreover, once the Highest in Heaven had assigned them to kill men while at the same time putting their own father's name on the list, the sons were in a most difficult position. And if they failed to find a substitute for their father, they did preserve his life with great ingenuity. It may be said that theirs was a change of form, not of heart.

The world is full of those who appear human and yet fail to recognize the king or the father standing in front of them. What, then, of those who have become tigers and yet remain grateful for the kindness they have enjoyed? How the Highest could let the boys' own father be on their list of victims is beyond me.

—*Hsü Fang*

🐾 Human Bait

Hsü Shan-ken of Shantung province made his living by digging ginseng roots, which are used in a precious tonic. Traditionally, ginseng diggers must do their work on the darkest possible nights. During one such night Hsü became exhausted from digging and went to sleep upon the sandy ground. He awoke to find himself clutched in the hand of a man some thirty feet tall who was covered all over with reddish hair. The giant was stroking Hsü Shan-ken and rubbing Hsü's body against his fur, as if he were playing with pearls or jade. At each stroke the giant burst into wild laughter, and Hsü reckoned that he was going to be the creature's next meal.

He felt himself being carried off. The giant took him to a cave containing mounds of such things as tiger sinew, deer tail, and elephant tusk. There the giant placed Hsü on a stone bed and offered him some tiger and deer meat. Although the ginseng digger was delighted to find that he was not himself going to be gobbled up, he could not eat the bloody chunks of flesh. The giant lowered his head as if he were thinking; then he nodded as if he understood. He struck a stone and made a fire, drew some water, and set a pot to boil. Cutting up the meat, he added it to the pot, and when the stew was ready the giant presented it to Hsü, who ate with relish.

As dawn approached, the giant took Hsü and five arrows and went out of the cave to the base of a cliff. There he tied Hsü to a tall tree and withdrew, leaving the ginseng digger terrified that the giant meant to shoot him. Presently a pack of tigers, scenting a live human, came out of caves in the cliffside. They jostled each other in their haste to get at Hsü, and the giant drew his arrows and killed them. Then he untied Hsü and carried him home in his arms, meanwhile dragging the dead tigers behind him. As before, he cooked them and offered his captive a feast

For more than a month Hsü served the giant as tiger bait. The ginseng digger came to no harm, and the giant grew quite fat. But one day Hsü became homesick and, kneeling before the giant, implored him tearfully, pointing again and again to the east. Weeping also, the giant took Hsü in his arms back to the place where he had been captured. He showed Hsü the way home and pointed out a number of choice ginseng patches. And that is how Hsü Shan-ken became a wealthy man.

—*Yüan Mei*

Educated Frogs
and Martial Ants

When I was young and living in Palm Lane, I saw a beggar who had a cloth sack and two bamboo tubes. In the sack he kept nine frogs. The tubes contained more than a thousand ants, some red and some white. He would go into a shop and display his act on the counter, then demand three coppers and leave.

One of his tricks was called "The Frog Teaches School." He set up a small chair, and a large frog leaped out of the sack and sat on it. Eight smaller frogs followed him out and formed a circle around the chair, sitting perfectly still. "Teach them!" the beggar cried. At once the large frog croaked, "Geggek." The class repeated in unison, "Geggek." And then all anyone could hear was "Geggek; geggek" until people's ears were ringing. So the beggar cried, "Stop!" At once all was quiet.

The other trick was called "Ants in Battle Formation." The beggar had two flags, one red, one white, each about a foot long. He emptied his bamboo tubes onto the counter, and the red and white ants scurried all over until he waved the red flag. "Form ranks!" he cried. The red ants formed themselves into a line. Next he waved the white flag and cried, "Form ranks!" The white ants did so too. Then he waved both flags and cried, "Mixed formation!" The ants mingled together and marched, turning left and right in perfect step. When they had made several rounds, he marched them back into the tubes.

Thus even such small dumb creatures as the frog and the ant can be taught, though I can't imagine how it is done.

—*Yüan Mei*

🐍 The Snakeman

A man of what is now Hopei province made his living by taming snakes and teaching them tricks. Once he raised and trained two black snakes: the larger he called Big Black; the smaller, Brother Black. Brother Black, who had red dots on his forehead, was very quick to learn his tricks. His twists and turns were exactly right, and the snakeman prized him above all the snakes he had owned.

After a year Big Black died. The snakeman wanted to replace him but had not yet found the time to do it when he took lodging one night in a mountain temple. He awoke in early dawn and opened his snake basket. Brother Black was missing! Calling frantically, the snakeman searched in the dim light, but there was no trace of the snake.

In the past whenever the snakeman had come upon a dense grove or thick vegetation, he stopped and let Brother Black free to enjoy himself. Brother Black always returned, so the snakeman had reason to hope that the snake would come back now. He sat down to wait, but when the sun had climbed high in the sky he despaired and left.

He had gone several paces away from the temple when he heard a low scraping sound in the depths of the thicket. Startled, he stopped and turned back. It was Brother Black! The snakeman felt overjoyed, as if he had regained a priceless jewel. He stopped to rest at a turn in the road, and the snake stopped also. When the snakeman looked again, he saw a small snake following Brother Black.

"I thought you were lost to me," said the snakeman, stroking Brother Black. "Are you presenting your little companion?" He

took out some food for Brother Black and his follower. The smaller snake curled up, too wild and shy to eat. So Brother Black fed the newcomer from his own mouth, in much the way that a host serves his guest first. The snakeman gave the small snake more food, and this time he ate for himself. When the meal was over, the small snake followed Brother Black into the basket.

The snakeman carried the basket off. And when the new snake began to learn tricks, he performed them all perfectly, just as Brother Black did. So the snakeman named the newcomer Baby Black. He took his act all over the country and made a handsome profit.

As a rule men who handle snakes have to discard them when

they grow more than two feet long, for they weigh too much to handle. The snakeman kept Brother Black as he grew beyond the limit because he was so tame. But after another couple of years the snake reached three feet and filled the basket entirely, so the snakeman decided to let him go.

One day when he came to the eastern hills of present-day Tsinan, the snakeman fed Brother Black something special, gave him his blessing, and freed him. The snake went off for a while but then returned and circled his basket. The snakeman shooed him away. "Be off! No party lasts forever, and the best of friends must part. Retire into the valley, and soon enough you are sure to become a divine dragon. Why do you want to remain in a basket?"

Brother Black wiggled away again, and the snakeman watched him go for a long time. But again the snake returned. When the snakeman shooed him away this time, he refused to leave and knocked his head against the basket. Baby Black was inside and becoming restless. Then it occurred to the snakeman that Brother Black must want to say goodbye to Baby Black. He opened the basket, and Baby Black came straight out and wrapped himself around Brother Black. Their tongues flickered as if they were talking to each other. Then they both went off in a carefree manner. The snakeman thought that Baby Black would not return, but after a while he undulated back in a sulky sort of way and finally crawled inside the basket.

The snakeman never again found a specimen so perfect as Brother Black. Meanwhile Baby Black was growing larger and unfit for handling. The snakeman acquired another snake that was rather tame but not the equal of Baby Black, who by this time was as thick as a child's arm.

When Brother Black first began to live in the hills, a number of woodmen saw him. Years later he had grown several feet and was as thick as a bowl. He began to come out and chase people. Travelers were soon warning one another, and no one dared enter the snake's territory. One day the snakeman was crossing the hills and a snake shot out at him like wind. Terrified, the snakeman ran. The snake pursued him and was about to overtake him when the snakeman saw the telltale red dots on his head.

"Brother Black! Brother Black!" cried the snakeman, setting down his burden. At once the snake stopped, lifted his head, and after a long while coiled himself around the snakeman, as he used to when they worked together. The snakeman realized that the snake meant no harm, but the reptile's body was so heavy that the man fell to the ground. He pleaded to be released, and the snake unwrapped himself and then knocked against the basket. Realizing what Brother Black wanted, the snakeman let Baby Black out.

When the two snakes met, they twisted around one another and clung tightly. After a lingering interval they separated. The snakeman gave his blessing to Baby Black. "For a long time I have wanted to let you go. Now you have a companion." To Brother Black he said, "You brought him to begin with, now you may take him away. One word more: There's plenty to eat in these hills. Don't disturb the travelers and suffer heaven's punishment."

The two snakes lowered their heads, as if accepting the admonition. Then they perked up and began to move, the elder in front, the younger following. Where they passed, branches split under their weight. The snakeman watched until he could see them no longer, then left. No one knows where the snakes went, but travelers had no further problems.

The snake, though a dumb creature, shows affection and loyalty to a friend. It is also readily teachable. How striking, in contrast, is he who seems human but throws away a ten-year friendship, or alienates a prince whose favor his family has enjoyed for generations; who dumps rocks on a wretch who has fallen down a well, or makes enemies of those who give him good advice!

—P'u Sung-ling

🌳 The North Country Wolf

Chien Tzu, the famous prince of Chao, was leading the great hunt in the northeast area of his state. The royal forester went ahead; hawks and hounds followed behind in order. And countless were the swift birds and fierce animals that fell as the bowstrings sang.

They came upon a wolf barring their way. It was standing up on its hind legs like a human, howling terribly. With ease and confidence, Chien Tzu leaped to the top of his chariot. He took his splendid bow and fitted to it a choice arrow made by the non-Chinese tribes of the north. Then he shot, and the arrow sank deep into the wolf. With a hoarse moan the wolf slipped away. Angered, Chien Tzu ordered his chariots to pursue. They kicked up enough dust to block the sky, and their hoofbeats boomed like thunder. At ten paces you could not tell man from horse.

Now, it happened that a scholar named Tung-kuo was on his way to the north country in search of official employment. Mr. Tung-kuo was a follower of the doctrine of Mo, which advocates universal love. Spurring a sorry ass forward, his bag loaded with all kinds of books, he had been traveling since early morning. Now he was lost and startled to see so much dust.

Suddenly the wolf arrived on the scene. Stretching its head forward, it eyed Mr. Tung-kuo keenly and said, "I believe, Master, that you are devoted to the salvation of all living things. In olden times Mao Pao freed a tortoise that later carried him over a river to safety. And the Marquis of Sui rescued a serpent that later brought him a priceless pearl. Now, who could doubt that a wolf can work more miracles than a tortoise or a serpent! So under the circumstances, couldn't you let me hide in your bag and prolong the bit of breath that's left to me? If some day I make good in this world, I shall give my all—no less than the tortoise or the serpent—to repay you for your kindness in saving me from certain death and keeping the flesh on my bones!"

"Aiya!" said the scholar. "If I show you this consideration and give offense to a high minister like Chien Tzu, flouting both authority and rank, you cannot imagine the trouble it would mean. There's no question of a reward from you to look forward to! Yet universal love is indeed the foundation of our Mohist doctrine. So after all, I should find some way to keep you alive. Whatever the danger, I cannot shirk the responsibility."

Mr. Tung-kuo removed his books from his bag, and when he had emptied it he gingerly began to pack the wolf inside. But first he tripped over his own feet and nearly stepped on the wolf's throat, and then he had trouble stuffing in the tail. After repeated efforts he still could not manage it. Mr. Tung-kuo paced back and forth in a quandary as the pursuing hunters drew closer.

"The situation is urgent," said the wolf. "Master, must one really preserve formalities when rescuing a drowning man, or let the chariot bells ring and give bandits a chance to escape? If only you would think of something quickly!" The scholar squeezed the wolf's four legs together, drew out a cord, and tied them tightly. Then he pushed the wolf's head down till it touched his tail, so that the animal's bent back protected its throat. Scrunched up like a porcupine, twisted around like a caterpillar, coiled in like a snake and breathing lightly as a tortoise, the wolf left his fate to the scholar.

As instructed, Mr. Tung-kuo put the wolf in his bag, pulled the opening tightly shut, and shouldered it onto the ass. Then he drew the ass to the left of the road to wait for the hunters to pass.

Soon Chien Tzu arrived. Not having found the wolf, he had worked himself into a great fury. With his sword he hacked off the end of the chariot's yoke and said, "The same for anyone who won't tell where the wolf went!"

The scholar flung himself on the ground in a posture of penance and crawled toward Chien Tzu on his hands and knees. Then, still kneeling, he raised himself and said, "My worthless, inept self, bold enough to come to these remote parts out of worldly ambition, has lost the right road. How, then, could I possibly make known the wolf's trail to Your Honor so that you may send your hawks and hounds after it? And yet there is the saying, 'The Great Way has many a side road for losing your sheep.' Even an animal like a sheep, so tame that a boy can tend it, still gets lost in the byroads. How unlike the sheep is the wolf, and how endless the byroads for losing sheep here in the north country! If you stick strictly to the main road in your search, isn't that practically the same as the folly of the farmer who waited by a tree stump for a hare to brain itself, or the folly of trying to get fish by climbing a tree? Anyway, hunting is your forester's job; my lord should ask his huntsmen. Why suspect a passing traveler? Besides, however unsophisticated my worthless self may be, I know wolves as well as the next man. They are greedy and fierce by nature, and no less cruel than the panther. Why, I would hustle myself into action and offer whatever service possible to help you get rid of one. How could you think I would conceal a wolf's whereabouts?"

Chien Tzu said nothing, turned his chariot around, and took to the road. Mr. Tung-kuo urged the ass forward in double time. It was a long, long while before the fledged poles of the hunting party faded away into the distance and the din of horse and chariot was heard no more. The wolf, surmising that Chien Tzu was now a good way off, spoke up from inside the bag, "Do not forget me, good Master. Get me out; untie the cord and pull the arrow from my side. Then I shall be going."

Mr. Tung-kuo released the wolf. The wolf gave out a raging roar and said to the scholar, "Just now the hunters were after me at full speed, and you kindly saved my life. But now I'm starving, and if I don't get any food I'm going to die all the same. I would have been better off slain by those hunters and gracing some nobleman's sacrificial vessel than dying here at the roadside and furnishing some wild beast with a meal. Since you're one of those altruistic Mohists who would wear himself to the bone to provide the world with a single benefit, why begrudge your single body to feed me and preserve my life?" And then, smacking his lips and flashing his claws, the wolf made for the scholar.

Mr. Tung-kuo frantically fended off the wolf with his bare hands. All the while he retreated until he could take cover behind the ass, which he then began to circle nimbly. The wolf never managed to get the better of the scholar, but the scholar spent all his energy escaping the wolf. The two of them, wilting with fatigue, panted for breath from opposite sides of the ass. "You have betrayed me," said the scholar, "betrayed me."

"Really, I didn't mean to," said the wolf, "but heaven has created your kind for the purpose of feeding ours." The man and the wolf held each other off a good long time, until the sun began to slant away. A dark thought occurred to the scholar: Night approaches. If wolves come in a pack, I shall be killed. So to deceive the wolf the scholar said, "It is the custom among humankind to inquire of three elders when a matter stands in doubt. Let us keep going and look for three elders to question. Should they agree that I deserve to be eaten, then you're welcome to me. If not, then let the matter be closed." The wolf was pleased with this, and the two of them went on.

They walked for a while, but not a traveler was to be seen. The wolf was starved. Ahead an old tree stood stiffly at the roadside. The wolf said, "Ask him!"

"Trees have no understanding," said Mr. Tung-kuo. "What's the good of asking a tree?"

"Just ask," said the wolf. "It should have something to say."

Having no choice, the scholar paid his respects to the tree and, after giving a full account of the situation, put the question to the tree, "So then, does the wolf have the right to eat me?"

A low rumbling came from within the tree. "I am an apricot," it said. "Years ago when the gardener planted me, all it cost him was a pit. In a few years I flowered. In another I bore fruit. After three years it took the full stretch of a man's hands to go around my trunk. After ten years it took the full length of a man's arms to embrace me. Now it is twenty years. I have fed the gardener. I have fed his wife. I have fed their guests. I have even fed their servants. And what's more, they made money selling my fruit in the market. You could say I have been of great service. But today I am old, no longer able to fold in my flowers and put forth my fruit, so I have earned the gardener's displeasure. He lops my branches and trims away my twigs and leaves. And now he even means to sell me to the carpenter for whatever money he can get. Oh Lord! Useless and old, I can find no mercy against the strokes of the axe. As for you, what favor have you done this wolf that you should hope for mercy? No question at all; he has the right to eat you."

When the apricot had delivered this opinion the wolf began to smack his lips and flex his claws once again as he headed for the scholar. "But you're breaking our agreement," said the scholar, "which was to put the question to *three* elders. So far we have come upon one apricot tree. Why should I be rushed?" So the two, man and wolf, resumed their journey.

The wolf was more frustrated than ever. In the distance he saw an old cow sunning itself beside a broken-down wall. "Ask this old one," said the wolf.

"That apricot tree had no sense or understanding," said the scholar. "Its absurd opinion has ruined everything. And this cow is nothing more than a beast. What more is gained in asking her?"

"Just ask," insisted the wolf, "or I gobble you up."

Having no choice, the scholar paid his respects to the old cow and recounted the whole story from beginning to end. Then he posed the question.

The cow wrinkled her forehead, unclosed her eyes, and licked her nose. Then she opened her mouth wide and said to the scholar, "The old apricot's opinion is not so wrong. When my horns were green stubs and my muscles good and firm, the farmer took me for the price of a knife and put me to work alongside the teams of oxen in his fields. After I grew to maturity, all the tasks fell to me because the others, the oxen, were growing weaker by the day. Whenever he decided to rush off somewhere, I bent my neck to the yoke and made haste on the chosen route. Whenever he wanted to plow, I was freed of the carriage yoke to amble off to the edge of his lands and clear away thorny brambles. I was as necessary as his own two hands. Thanks to me he had his basic sustenance; marriage ceremonies could be carried out, taxes could be paid, the granary stood full. You would think I'd at least have a stall for shelter, like the horse or the dog!

"In the old days the family never put more than a stone of grain in store. Now they're taking in over one hundred pecks of wheat. In the old days they were too poor for people to notice them. Now he marches grandly through village society. In the old days poverty left their winecups dusty and their lips dry, for never in their lives could they afford a full winejar. Now he ferments fine millet, holds an ornamental winepot, and boasts a wife and concubines. In the old days their clothes were coarse and short, and he kept company with trees and stones. His hands were as unaccustomed to ceremonial salutes as his mind to learning. Now he has a primer in hand, sports a bamboo hat, wears a tanned leather belt, and has ample full-length garments. Every thread, every grain—my labor. And in my old age he abuses me and drives me into the wilds, where the raw wind stings my eyes. In the chill daylight I grieve to see my shadow, so thin that the bones stick up like hills, so old that my tears are rain. I cannot hold in my spittle. My legs are too crippled to raise. My hide and hair are patchy. My sores never heal.

"The farmer's wife, that jealous, vicious woman, is always putting forward her view: 'Every part of a cow's body is useful,' says she. 'The flesh can be preserved dry. The hide can go for leather. Even bones and horns can be carved into utensils.' Then she'll point to the eldest son. 'You've been training,' says she, 'under the finest butchers for years. How about sharpening your blade and disposing of her?' These signs bode no good for me. Who knows where I will lie down for good? I may have much to my credit, but they are so heartless that calamity is coming soon. As for you, what favor have you done this wolf that you should expect mercy?"

When the cow had delivered her opinion, the wolf smacked his lips, flexed his claws, and headed for the scholar. "Not so fast!" said the scholar. In the distance an old man was approaching, leaning on a goosefoot staff. His beard and eyebrows were pure white; his dress was casual but elegant. He looked like a cultivated man, a sage of the Tao. Delighted, Mr. Tung-kuo went up to the old man and kneeled before him respectfully. Weeping, he stated his case.

"I beg of you, good sir, the word that will save me." The old man asked what the matter was, and the scholar continued, "This wolf was almost caught by the royal hunters when it turned to me for help. And in fact I enabled it to stay alive. But now, deaf to my entreaties, it wants to make a meal of me. My life is forfeit if the wolf does not relent. I sought a brief delay during which we agreed to let three elders decide the matter. First we met an old apricot tree, to which he forced me to submit the question. Trees have no understanding, and its answer nearly cost me my life. Next we met an old cow. Again the wolf forced me to seek her answer. Animals have no understanding either, and again I nearly lost my life. Now we meet with you, good sir. It can only mean that heaven does not intend to let learning perish, as Confucius put it. Do I dare to beg for the word that saves me?" The scholar pressed his forehead to the ground in front of the old man's staff, and there he remained, awaiting his fate.

The elder sighed again and again as he listened to the whole story. Then he knocked the wolf with his staff, saying, "You are in the wrong. Among men nothing is more accursed than to betray a benefactor. The Confucians have always held that a man who could not bear to betray his benefactor was sure to be a filial son. The Confucians also claim that even the tiger and the wolf acknowledge the bond between father and son. But now that you have turned on your benefactor like this, even the bond between father and son does not exist for you. Begone, wolf!" the old man screamed. "Or I shall beat you to death."

"Good sir," replied the wolf, "to quote Confucius, 'You may know the first part, but you have yet to learn the second.' Allow me to explain, if you would condescend to listen. When all this began, the scholar saved my life by tying up my four feet, hiding me in his bag, and loading his 'classics' on top of me. I curled myself up, not daring to breathe. In addition, he went on and on trying to convince Chien Tzu of his innocence with the apparent intention of letting me die in the bag and stealing all the glory for himself! Why shouldn't I eat him up for this?"

The elder looked hard at the scholar and said, "Well, if that's the case, then you're to blame—just like the ancient archer Yi who taught all he knew to the man who later killed him." Feeling deeply wronged, the scholar described in detail his compassionate intent in putting the wolf in his bag. But the wolf also strove to win the argument with great cunning.

"I am afraid neither of you is fully convincing," said the elder. "Try putting the wolf back into the bag so I can see what it was like and whether it was really as painful as the wolf says."

The wolf was only too glad to do so. He stretched his legs towards the scholar, who tied him up and put him in the bag once again. Then Mr. Tung-kuo shouldered the bag up onto the ass. The wolf did not know what was going on. "Have you a knife?" the elder whispered to the scholar.

"Yes," he replied and drew it out. The elder signaled with a glance for the scholar to stab the wolf.

"Won't that hurt him?" asked the scholar.

Smiling, the elder replied, "Still 'can't bear to kill' even such a treacherous beast? You may be humane, but your foolishness is greater. If you go down a well to save someone, or take off your clothes to keep a friend alive, it may be to the other's advantage, but what's the point of dying in the bargain? Are you one of *that* sort? Surely no gentleman and scholar approves compassion that descends to folly." So saying, the elder laughed loudly, and so did the scholar. The elder helped the scholar with the knife, and together they put the wolf to death, threw his body on the road, and left.

—*Ma Chung-hsi*

❧ Counselor to the Wolves

A man named Ch'ien went to the market and was walking home late at the foot of the hills when several dozen wolves sprang out. They made a hungry circle around him. Desperate, Ch'ien saw a pile of firewood more than ten feet high by the side of the road and swiftly clambered to the top. None of the wolves could climb it. But a few of them ran off and returned in a short while escorting an animal, much the way porters ferry an official in a sedan-chair.

The crowd of wolves bent their ears to the animal's mouth as if he were imparting secrets. Next they leaped up and began pulling branches from the bottom of the woodpile. Soon the whole pile was about to collapse. Panicking, Ch'ien cried for help. By chance some woodcutters heard his voice and came shouting.

The wolves fled in fright, leaving behind the animal they had brought. Ch'ien and the woodsmen looked it over carefully. It resembled a wolf but was not a wolf. It had round eyes, a short neck, a long snout, and fearsome teeth. Its back legs were long but weak, and it could not stand on them. Its cry was like a gibbon's howl.

Ch'ien spoke to it: "You and I are no enemies! Why did you serve the wolves as strategist in their attempt to kill me?"

The beast knocked its head against the ground and wailed as if repenting. The men dragged it to a wineshop in the village ahead, cooked it, and had it for dinner.

—Yüan Mei

 # Monkey Keeper

In the land of Sung there was a monkey keeper who loved monkeys. He raised a whole swarm of them and could understand their thoughts. They were so dear to him that he would take food from the mouths of his own family to satisfy them. But still the time came when he had to reduce their provisions. Fearing that they would stop obeying him, he decided to trick them into accepting short rations. "Here are chestnuts for you," he told them. "You'll get three each morning and four each evening. Is that enough?" The monkeys rose up in anger. Then the trainer said, "Very well; four each morning and three each evening. Is that enough?" Delighted, the monkeys agreed.

—*Lieh Tzu*

Man and Beast

The leader of the T'ien clan was preparing a grand feast for a thousand guests. At the place of honor someone presented an offering of fish and wild geese. The clan leader examined the offering and sighed, "How generous heaven is to the people, growing the five grains and breeding fish and fowl for us to use." The whole assembly echoed their leader's voice.

A boy of twelve, a son of the Pao clan who was present in the ranks, stepped forward and said, "Not at all! Heaven and earth and the ten thousand things between are born as one with us, alike in kind to us. There is no high and low among the kinds. It is merely that one kind dominates another by virtue of size or strength or wit. And so one devours the other and is devoured in turn. But heaven did not create things *for* each other. Man eats whatever he can, but did heaven breed what man eats specifically for man? The mosquito and the gnat bite man's skin, the tiger and the wolf feed on flesh. Has heaven created man for the mosquito, or flesh for the tiger and the wolf?"

—*Lieh Tzu*

🌸 Man or Beast

Those alike in mind may differ in form. Those alike in form may differ in mind. The sage prefers what is like-minded and ignores what is alike in form. Ordinary men stick close to what is alike in form and keep their distance from what is like-minded. "We cherish and cling to what resembles us," they say.

That which has a six-foot frame, two hands and two feet, hair on top and teeth in the mouth, and moves upright—ordinary men call human. But it is not impossible for a man to have a beast's heart. Yet if he does, he will still be treated well because of his human form. What is winged or horned, has spaced teeth and spread claws, and flies or prowls—ordinary men call a beast. But it is not impossible for a beast to have a human heart. Yet if it does, men will still shun it because of its looks.

The great gods of old (Pao Hsi, who tamed wild animals and sacrificed them in fire; Nü Wa, who repaired the skies and molded the race of men; Shen Neng, the divine farmer who founded agriculture and medicine; the Hsia rulers, who established the first dynasty) all had the body of a reptile with a human face, or an ox's head, or a tiger's snout. None looked human, though they were sages of great virtue.

But the infamous kings of later times (Chieh, who ruined the first dynasty; Chou, who ruined the second dynasty of Shang; Huan, who destroyed the law of succession in Lu; and King Mu of Ch'u, who rebelled and slew his sovereign) all had ears, eyes, nose, and mouth—the seven apertures of the human face—but the hearts of beasts. Ordinary men cling to a single appearance in search of the highest wisdom and never reach it.

The Yellow God-king of the north fought the southern God-king of Fire in the wilderness of Fanch'uan. In the vanguard the Yellow God-king led bears, grizzlies, leopards, saber-toothed and common tigers. Buzzards, ospreys, falcons, and hawks served as flag and signal bearers. Thus the Yellow God-king had power to make birds and beasts fight for him.

The sage-king Yao put K'uei in charge of music. K'uei struck the chime-stones sharply and softly, and all the animals danced in order. When the ancient royal wind music of Shao was performed, the sacred phoenix presented itself with ceremonial grandeur. Thus the sound of music brought bird and beast under Yao's influence. How, then, does the mind of these creatures differ from man's? The difference is one of outer shape and speech only. But man has lost the art of communicating with them. Only the sage, with his wide knowledge and thorough comprehension, is able to lead them into his service.

The natural faculty of self-preservation is common to beasts and to man; beasts do not learn it from man. Male and female pair. Mother and child hug. Beasts avoid the open and keep to rough terrain. They shun cold and seek warmth. When they are settled, they herd; on the move, they form ranks with the weakest on the inside, the strongest on the outside. Whenever one of them finds water, he leads the others to it; whenever one of them finds food, he calls the herd. In the most ancient days the beasts lived and moved alongside man. Only in the reign of emperors and kings did they disperse in fear. And now in our own evil times, they lurk in dark places or scurry for safety lest man slay them.

Today in the eastern land of the Chieh tribe, the people have a special gift for understanding the speech of domesticated animals. But the sacred sages of ancient times knew all there was to know about the natures of things. They understood the cries and calls of different species, gathered them in assembly, and taught them as if they were people. Indeed, first the sages would bring together the spirits of the dead and other demons, next they would gather the peoples of the eight outlying directions, lastly they would assemble the beasts and insects for their lessons. This shows that all species which have blood and breath do not differ much in their hearts and minds. The holy sages knew this well, and that is why they taught all and left none out.

—Lieh Tzu

🌸 The Fish Rejoice

Chuang Tzu and his close friend Hui Tzu were out enjoying each other's company on the shores of the Hao. Chuang Tzu said, "The flashing fish are out enjoying each other, too, swimming gracefully this way and that. Such is their joy!"

"You're no fish," said Hui Tzu. "How can you tell they are enjoying themselves?"

"You're no Chuang Tzu," said Chuang Tzu. "How can you tell I can't tell?"

"As surely as 'I'm no Chuang Tzu' proves *I* can't tell," said Hui Tzu, " 'You're no fish' proves *you* can't tell. It's perfectly logical."

"May we begin at the beginning?" returned Chuang Tzu. "By asking 'How can you tell the fish are enjoying themselves?' you acknowledged I could tell you! And what's more I can do it from up here!"

—*Chuang Tzu*

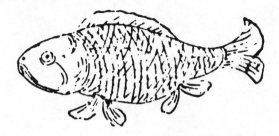

Wagging My Tail in the Mud

The hermit poet Chuang Tzu was angling in the River Pu. The king of Ch'u sent two noblemen to invite Chuang to come before him. "We were hoping you would take on certain affairs of state," they said. Holding his pole steady and without looking at them, Chuang Tzu said, "I hear Ch'u has a sacred tortoise that has been dead three thousand years, and the king has it enshrined in a cushioned box in the ancestral hall. Do you think the tortoise would be happier wagging his tail in the mud than having his shell honored?" "Of course," replied the two noblemen. "Then begone," said Chuang Tzu. "I mean to keep wagging mine in the mud."

—*Chuang Tzu*

WOMEN
AND WIVES

Li Chi Slays the Serpent

In Fukien, in the ancient state of Yüeh, stands the Yung mountain range, whose peaks sometimes reach a height of many miles. To the northwest there is a cleft in the mountains once inhabited by a giant serpent seventy or eighty feet long and wider than the span of ten hands. It kept the local people in a state of constant terror and had already killed many commandants from the capital city and many magistrates and officers of nearby towns. Offerings of oxen and sheep did not appease the monster. By entering men's dreams and making its wishes known through mediums, it demanded young girls of twelve or thirteen to feast on.

Helpless, the commandant and the magistrates selected daughters of bondmaids or criminals and kept them until the appointed dates. One day in the eighth month of every year, they would deliver a girl to the mouth of the monster's cave, and the serpent would come out and swallow the victim. This continued for nine years until nine girls had been devoured.

In the tenth year the officials had again begun to look for a girl to hold in readiness for the appointed time. A man of Chianglo county, Li Tan, had raised six daughters and no sons. Chi, his youngest girl, responded to the search for a victim by volunteering. Her parents refused to allow it, but she said, "Dear parents, you have no one to depend on, for having brought forth six daughters and not a single son, it is as if you were childless. I could never compare with Ti Jung of the Han Dynasty, who of-

fered herself as a bondmaid to the emperor in exchange for her father's life. I cannot take care of you in your old age; I only waste your good food and clothes. Since I'm no use to you alive, why shouldn't I give up my life a little sooner? What could be wrong in selling me to gain a bit of money for yourselves?" But the father and mother loved her too much to consent, so she went in secret.

The volunteer then asked the authorities for a sharp sword and a snake-hunting dog. When the appointed day of the eighth month arrived, she seated herself in the temple, clutching the sword and leading the dog. First she took several pecks of rice balls moistened with malt sugar and placed them at the mouth of the serpent's cave.

The serpent appeared. Its head was as large as a rice barrel; its eyes were like mirrors two feet across. Smelling the fragrance of the rice balls, it opened its mouth to eat them. Then Li Chi unleashed the snake-hunting dog, which bit hard into the serpent. Li Chi herself came up from behind and scored the serpent with several deep cuts. The wounds hurt so terribly that the monster leaped into the open and died.

Li Chi went into the serpent's cave and recovered the skulls of the nine victims. She sighed as she brought them out, saying, "For your timidity you were devoured. How pitiful!" Slowly she made her way homeward.

The king of Yüeh learned of these events and made Li Chi his queen. He appointed her father magistrate of Chiang Lo county, and her mother and elder sisters were given riches. From that time forth, the district was free of monsters. Ballads celebrating Li Chi survive to this day.

—*Kan Pao*

The Black General

Kuo Yüan-chen, who later became the lord of Tai, failed the official examination during the K'ai Yüan era (A.D. 713–742). Afterwards, while traveling, he lost his way in the night. A good while later he saw the rays of a light far, far away, and assuming that it was a dwelling, headed toward it.

He rode some three miles until he reached a tall and imposing structure. In the corridors and the main hall, lanterns and candles were blazing brightly as he entered. Delicacies and sacrificial meats were laid out as in the home of a family whose daughter was to wed. Yet it was silent and deserted.

Kuo tied his horse outside the west corridor and climbed the steps. In the hall he hesitated, not knowing where he was. Presently from the east chamber he heard the sound of a girl sobbing uncontrollably. "Is it human or ghost who cries in this house?" Kuo called. "And why is the hall so splendidly arrayed, with no one here but you alone in tears?"

"There is a temple in my village," she replied, "for the Black General, who can bring men good fortune or ill. Each year he demands a mate from the villagers, and from the local virgins they select a beauty to be his bride. Though I am ugly, my father stood to gain five hundred strings of cash from the villagers by secretly agreeing to my selection. This evening the young girls of the village, my friends and companions, made me drunk in this room, then locked me in and left, leaving me to wed the demon. My father and mother have abandoned me. Nothing remains for

me but death. I am beside myself with grief and terror. Sir, are
you a real man? Can you rescue me? For the rest of my life I
would be your obedient servant."

"When do you expect this 'General'?" asked Kuo, indignant.

"At the second watch."

"I am a man—if I may say so—and will do all I can to save you.
If I fail, I shall sacrifice my life instead. For I would never allow
you to suffer death at the hands of this lewd demon!"

The girl's sobs subsided. Kuo seated himself in the west hall-
way and moved his horse to the north of the building. He also
assigned a servant to stand in front of him and wait like a master
of ceremonies receiving guests.

Soon there was a blaze of torches and hubbub of horses and
carriage. Two purple-robed servants entered the building and
walked out again, saying, "The prime minister is in there!" Then
two yellow-robed servants entered timidly and again went out,
saying, "The prime minister is in there!" Kuo was inwardly gratified and thought to himself, "If I am destined to become prime
minister, I know I will overcome this demon!"

Then the "General" himself slowly descended from his carriage, and the heralds again reported to him. "Enter!" said the
General. With that he strode in, surrounded by armed attendants, and went to the foot of the steps leading to the east chamber. Kuo ordered his servant to step forward and announce,
"Master Kuo presents himself." Then Kuo himself made a formal
salutation.

"How does Master Kuo come to be here?" asked the General.

"I had heard of the General's wedding this evening and was
hoping to be of assistance in the ceremony," answered Kuo.

Pleased, the one known as General invited Kuo to take a place
at the table. They sat opposite one another, their speech and
laughter cordial. Kuo had a sharp knife in his bag which he
thought he would use to kill the Black General, so he asked,
"Have you ever tasted preserved venison?"

"It would be hard to find in a place like this," said the General.

"I have a small supply of choice quality," said Kuo. "It comes
from the imperial kitchen. May I slice some for you?"

The General was delighted. Kuo got up, took the venison and
his small knife, and began slicing it. He set a plate before the
General and asked him to help himself. Unsuspicious, the Gen-

eral reached for the meat. Quickly Kuo threw down the venison, seized the General's wrist, and cut off his hand.

With a shriek the Black General fled. His followers scattered in terror. Kuo took the severed hand and wrapped it in a piece of his own clothing. Then he sent the servant outside to reconnoiter; the grounds were deserted. He opened the door of the east chamber and said to the tearful young girl, "I have here the hand of the Black General. We will follow the trail of blood, and soon he will be done for. Now that you are safe, come out and help yourself to some food."

The tearful lass came out. She was only seventeen or eighteen, and most attractive. Bowing to Kuo, she said, "I swore to become your servant." Kuo consoled and comforted her. As day was about to dawn, he unwrapped the hand and saw that it was a black pig's foot. Presently they heard sounds of cries and sobs gradually approaching. It was the girl's kinfolk and the village elders, bearing a coffin to take the girl's body for burial.

When they saw Kuo with the young maid still alive, they were amazed and questioned him. Then the elders grew angry because he had injured their local divinity. "The Black General is a god that guards this village," they said, "and we have served him for a long time. Each year we offer him one of our young maids as a mate, and we keep safe and sound by doing so. If the ritual should be delayed, we will suffer storm and hail. By what right does a stranger who has lost his way come to harm our illustrious god and bring down on us his divine violence? What has our village ever done to you to deserve this? You ought to be killed and offered to the Black General, or bound and delivered to our magistrate!"

They were about to order their young men to seize Kuo when he began to admonish them. "You people are old in years but not in experience. I am one who is acquainted with the ways of the world. Listen to what I have to say. When a god receives the mandate of heaven to protect an area, is it not the same as a territorial lord receiving the mandate of the emperor to govern his domain?"

"Yes, it is," they agreed.

"Now then, suppose the territorial lord were angling for illicit pleasures in his realm; would not the emperor be angry? And if that lord were cruel to the people, would not the emperor punish him?

"Is he whom you call General a real divinity? Surely no divinity has a pig's foot! Has heaven ever given its mandate to a lustful demonic beast? Indeed, is not such a beast a criminal in heaven as well as on earth?

"I had the right when I punished the fiend. How could this be wrong? There is no righteous man among you, if you could send your tender girls to a violent death at the hands of a demon year after year! Can you be sure heaven has not sent me to redress these crimes?

"Accept what I say, and I will rid you of the demon so that you will never again have to deliver a bride to it. What do you say?"

The villagers realized that this was the truth and were only too happy to accept Kuo's leadership. Kuo ordered several hundred men to take bows and arrows, swords and spears, spades and hoes, and to follow him in a group. They pursued the trail of blood left by the Black General, and after about seven miles it led to the burial chamber of a large tomb. They formed a circle and hacked at it. The opening began to widen. When it was as wide as the mouth of a large jar, Kuo ordered bundles of firewood to be kindled and thrown inside so they could see. The interior was like a large chamber. They saw a giant swine missing its left forefoot lying in a pool of blood. Dashing out of the smoke, it was killed by the encircling men.

The villagers rejoiced with one another. They collected a farewell gift to thank Kuo, but he refused it, saying, "In fighting evil for the people, I seek no gain." The maiden who had been rescued bid goodbye to her parents and kinsmen, saying, "I was fortunate to be born a human being and your own flesh and blood. I had never even been out of my chambers and surely committed no offense deserving death. Yet for the gain of five hundred strings of copper, I was to be married off to a demon. You were hard-hearted enough to lock me up and leave me behind. Is that what human beings ought to do? If it were not for Master Kuo's courage and humanity, I wouldn't be here today. He gave me life; my parents gave me death. It is my wish to go with Master Kuo and never give another thought to my old home." Tearfully bowing, she followed Kuo and would not be dissuaded, so he took her as his concubine and she bore him several sons.

Kuo's official career was one of uninterrupted high position, as the Black General's demon-servants had foreseen. Though he was born in a remote part of the country and failed in the official examinations, the spirits could not harm a wise and righteous man.

—Niu Seng-ju

✿The Master and the Serving Maid

To decide right and wrong, we have only tradition and law to go by. And yet there are cases where people single-mindedly follow their convictions without the approval of tradition or sanction of law.

In my own clan there was a serving maid named Liu Ch'ing. When she was seven her master ordered that she be given in marriage to a young servant named Yi Shou. When she was sixteen a day was set for the wedding. But suddenly Yi Shou ran away because of some gambling debts, and for a long time there was no news of him. The master was ready to match Liu Ch'ing with another servant, but she swore to die before she would agree.

Liu Ch'ing was rather appealing, and the master himself tried to interest her in becoming his concubine. Again she swore to die before she would agree. The master sent an older woman to talk her into it. The woman told her, "Even if you're not going to give up on Yi Shou, you might as well accept the master for now. Meanwhile we'll do all we can to find Yi Shou and marry you to him. If you refuse, you'll be sold away to some remote area and lose all chance of seeing Yi Shou again."

For a few days Liu Ch'ing cried silently. Then with head bowed low, she offered her pillow to the master. But she kept insisting

that the search for Yi Shou go on. Three or four years later, Yi Shou returned to accept his fate and settle his debts. True to his word, the master ordered the nuptials.

After the wedding the serving maid resumed her duties, but she never exchanged another word with the master. She promptly avoided his slightest approach. He had her whipped and gave Yi Shou money to coerce her, but she firmly refused any relations with the master. In the end the master had no choice but to send them away with his blessing.

As Liu Ch'ing was getting ready to leave, she placed a small box before the master's mother. Then she departed, touching her head to the floor in respectful submission. When the box was opened, they found all the personal gifts the master had made her over the years. Not a thing was missing.

Later Yi Shou became a peddler, while Liu Ch'ing took in sewing to survive. But she had no regrets to her dying day.

When I was living at home, Yi Shou was still trading in brass and ceramic utensils. His hair had gone white. I asked him about his wife. "Dead," he replied.

Strange! this serving maid neither chaste nor unchaste, both chaste and unchaste! I see no way to unriddle it, so I made this record for more learned gentlemen to judge.

—*Chi Yün*

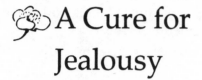# A Cure for Jealousy

The young scholar Hsien-yüan of Changchou was childless at thirty. His wife, a woman of the Chang clan, was abnormally jealous, and Hsien-yüan was too afraid of her to take a second wife who might bear him the sons he wanted. Chancellor Ma of the Grand Secretariat, the presiding official at Hsien-yüan's degree examination, felt sorry for the young man and presented him with a concubine. First Wife Chang was furious at this intrusion into her family affairs and swore to repay Chancellor Ma in kind.

It happened around then that Chancellor Ma lost his own wife. So Lady Chang found a country woman widely known for her bad temper and bribed a go-between to persuade Ma to make the shrew his new first wife. The Chancellor saw through Chang's scheme but proceeded with the betrothal. On the wedding day the trousseau included a five-colored club for the purpose of beating husbands. It was an heirloom that had been in the country woman's family for three generations.

When the wedding ceremony ended, Ma's host of concubines offered their respects. The new first wife asked who all these women were, and they told her that they were concubines. The bride lashed out, "What social law sanctions concubines in the household of a dignified chancellor?" She took the club to attack the women, but Chancellor Ma ordered them to seize it and beat the wife instead. She fled to her room cursing and crying, while the concubines created such a din with gongs and drums that her sobs could not be heard.

The new wife then declared that she would do away with herself. Promptly offering her a knife and a rope, the attendants said, "The master has been expecting you to try something like this. So he has given us these dreadful things to present to you." At that the concubines beat upon wooden drums and chanted the mantra so that her soul would ascend quickly to paradise. They made such a racket that the first wife's ravings about taking her own life were not heard.

Chancellor Ma's new first wife was basically a woman of dignity. Realizing that she had exhausted her bluffs and threats, she conquered her anger and called for the Chancellor. Putting on a proper expression when he entered her room, she said, "My lord, you are truly a man! The tricks I have been using were handed down from my great-grandmother—effective, perhaps, for intimidating the spineless men of this world, but not the way to treat you, my lord. I want to serve you from now on. And I hope that you for your part will treat me according to propriety."

"If it can be so," replied the Chancellor, "so be it." And they saluted one another again as bride and groom. Chancellor Ma ordered the concubines to apologize by knocking their heads to the floor. Then he put his first wife in charge of all money and gems and of the account books for their fields and dwellings. And in a month's time the Ma household was orderly and harmonious. There was no criticism from inside or out.

Now Chang, the first wife of Hsien-yüan, having sent one of her followers to Chancellor Ma's wedding, learned all about the confrontation between the first wife and the concubines. "Why didn't she beat them with her club?" asked Chang.

"She was overpowered."

"Why didn't she curse and cry?"

"The noise of their drums and the clamor of their voices drowned her out."

"Why didn't she threaten suicide?"

"They had knife and rope all ready, and they sang the mantra for rebirth to bid her farewell."

"What did the new first wife do then?"

"She submitted to good form and gave in."

Enraged, Lady Chang exclaimed, "For the world to have such a good-for-nothing woman! She has spoiled everything."

Now when Chancellor Ma had first presented the concubine to Hsien-yüan, Hsien-yüan's classmates prepared lamb and wines and went to congratulate him. As soon as everyone at the party was feeling mellow, Lady Chang began abusing the guests from behind a screen. Everyone bore her insults impassively, except for one classmate who was a habitual drunkard. He stepped forward, seized Lady Chang by the hair, and slapped her. "If you show respect to my elder brother Hsien-yüan, you are my sister-in-law," he said; "otherwise you are my enemy. Your husband was childless, and that is why his examiner and patron, Chancellor Ma, presented him with a concubine. He was thinking of the future of your ancestral line. One word more, and you die under my fist!" The other guests rushed forward and pulled the man off her so that she could escape. But she was humiliated, for her skirts were torn and some clothing was damaged, nearly exposing parts of her body.

Lady Chang had been nicknamed the Female Demon. With her ferocious pride badly hurt by the turn of events, her hatred of Chancellor Ma increased. She expressed it by doing everything she could to make life miserable for the concubine he had presented. But the concubine, who still received secret instructions from the Chancellor, remained compliant and agreeable. Though she was now a part of the household, she never exchanged a word with Hsien-yüan. For this reason Lady Chang stopped short of having her put to death.

In a short while Chancellor Ma personally presented one hundred pieces of silver to Hsien-yüan. "Next spring," he told his protégé, "there will be a triennial examination for the highest degree. Take this for your expenses and go to the capital now, so that you can spend the next few months in study."

Hsien-yüan accepted the gift and went home to tell Lady Chang that he was leaving. Since she had been worried that he would become intimate with the concubine, the first wife was only too glad to bid him goodbye.

As Hsien-yüan was boarding the boat to the capital, however, one of Chancellor Ma's servants intercepted him and took him to Ma's own home. There in the seclusion of the back gardens, the young man pursued his studies in peace.

At the same time, Chancellor Ma sent a go-between to persuade Lady Chang that she should take advantage of Hsien-yüan's absence and sell the concubine. "That's what I'd like to do," said Lady Chang, "but it must be to a buyer in a remote place, so there will be no problems later on." "No problem at all," said the go-between.

Presently a cloth seller from Shensi province came to see Lady Chang. He was ugly and bearded but carried three hundred pieces of silver. Chang summoned the young concubine, who pleased the traveling salesman no end. The bargain was struck, but Lady Chang was not satisfied until she had stripped the gown and shoes from the concubine. Now poorly clothed, without even a hairpin in the way of finery, the concubine was put into a bamboo sedan chair and taken off. As the porters carried her over the north bridge, she cried out, "I won't go so far away," and she jumped into the water. (However, a small boat darted out, picked up the concubine, and ferried her to Ma's rear garden, where she joined Hsien-yüan.)

When Lady Chang heard that the girl had drowned, she fell into a state of fright and confusion. Then the salesman from Shensi burst in on her and raged: "I bought a live woman, not a dead one. You sold her without making the situation clear to her. How dare you force a good woman to do something mean? You have taken advantage of a simple traveler. Give me back my money." Having no defense, Lady Chang returned his three hundred pieces of silver.

The following day a man and a woman, white-headed and tattered, appeared at Lady Chang's house. "Chancellor Ma took our daughter and presented her to your household as a concubine," they wailed. "Where is she now? If she lives, return her. If she is dead, return the body." Lady Chang had no answer. The two old parents knocked their heads against Lady Chang, ready to give up their own lives. They threw plates and smashed bowls until not an article in the household was left unbroken. They would not leave until Chang gave them money and her neighbors interceded and begged them to go.

Another day, four or five fierce constables from the county magistrate came carrying the official crimson arrest warrant. "This is a case involving human life," they said. "We must conduct the culprit Chang to appear before the magistrate." They threw their iron chains on the table with a resounding clang. Lady Chang asked the reason, but they would say nothing. When she offered them money, however, they told her that a certain concubine's parents had reported the suspicious death of their daughter.

Lady Chang was now terrified, and she wished that her husband were at home to deal with these things so that she, a lone woman, would not be shamed and made to stand up in court. She keenly regretted her bad treatment of her husband, her violence toward the concubine, the mistakes she had made, and the helplessness of being a woman. She was torn between resentment and remorse when someone dashed up wearing the white mourning cap. "Master Hsien-yüan has died suddenly at the Lu Kou Bridge," he shouted. "I am the muleteer; I came straightaway to tell you."

Lady Chang was too shaken to speak. "We had better go," said the constables to each other, "since there has been a death in the family." Lady Chang went to prepare her costume for the funeral. A few days later the constables came again, and Chang engaged a lawyer to assist her. She pawned her trousseau and sold the house to bribe the court clerk to delay her case. This gave her a respite, but now she was bankrupt and could not even buy food.

Again the go-between arrived and said, "Madame is in such straits—and without a son to raise in widowhood!"

Lady Chang was so distressed that she went to a blind fortune teller. The woman cast Chang's horoscope and said, "It is your fate to wive two men. Wearing gold and pearl, you will marry again."

After hearing this, Lady Chang summoned the go-between and told her, "I would be willing to remarry; destiny cannot be avoided. But since I am arranging my own marriage, I must see the groom first." The go-between brought a handsome, splendidly dressed young man for her inspection. "That is Master So-and-So," she said.

The delighted Lady Chang put off her widow's weeds and married the youth before the end of the forty-nine-day mourning period. As the couple were performing the wedding ritual of sharing the cup, an ugly woman wielding a large club rushed out of the house. "I am the formal wife and mistress here!" she screeched. "How dare you come into my home as a concubine! I won't allow it!" She beat Lady Chang severely, and Lady Chang regretted having been deceived by the go-between even as she realized that this was exactly how she had treated Hsien-yüan's concubine. "Is that the will of heaven?" she wondered. Her tears fell silently.

Guests and friends finally persuaded the first wife to stop. "Let the young master consummate the wedding," they said, "and save the complaints for tomorrow."

Several youths holding wedding candles escorted Lady Chang to the bedroom. No sooner was the screen raised than lo! Hsien-yüan himself was sitting grandly upon the bed. Certain that he was reappearing as a ghost, Lady Chang fell to the ground in a faint. When she returned to consciousness, she pleaded through her tears, "Do not think I have betrayed you, my lord; truly I had no choice."

With a laugh Hsien-yüan waved his hand. "Have no fear. Have no fear," he said. "Your two marriages are still one marriage." Then he put her on the bed and told her how she had been taken in by Chancellor Ma's scheme. At first she could not believe it, but soon everything became clear to her. She felt remorse and shame, and from then on she reformed her conduct. In fact, both Lady Chang and the country woman whom Chancellor Ma had married turned to the paths of virtue and became worthy wives forever after.

—Yüan Mei

🥮 The Fortune Teller

District Superintendent Chao told this story about a Superintendent Li in the capital. Li was a third-rank official of great wealth and status, but he was well into his fifties and had no son. He had heard that east of the emperor's council headquarters there was a magician who was running a fortune-telling room and making amazing and accurate predictions. Superintendent Li decided to see if the man could tell him whether he would have a son.

"I am interested neither in money nor in long life. I only want to know if I am to have a son."

The fortune teller smiled and replied, "You already have one. Are you trying to put something over on me?"

"The truth is, I have none," said Li. "How could I be putting something over on you?"

The fortune teller became angry and said, "You must have had a son when you were forty years old. Now you are fifty-six. What *are* you doing, if not putting something over?"

Many of the army men sitting around were amazed to see the two of them arguing. Then Superintendent Li thought long and quietly to himself before saying to the fortune teller, "When I was forty, one of my serving maids became pregnant. At the time I had to go north to the Mongol capital on official business. When I came home, my wife had already sold the maid. No one knows where she went, but if she had a son, he must be mine."

"He will be returned to you," said the fortune teller. Li bid the man goodbye and left.

A legion commander who had witnessed all this took Superintendent Li to a tea shop and told him, "Fifteen years ago, I too had no son. I went to the capital to arrange for a concubine, and it happened that the woman was already pregnant. When I returned home with her, my wife was with child. Each gave birth to a son hardly a month apart. Now the boys are sixteen. Could one of them be yours?"

The descriptions the two men gave of the concubine agreed. Li went home to speak to his wife who, though she had once been cruel and jealous, was softened now from regret that they had no heir. The next day they invited the commander to their home and laid a sumptuous feast for him. They set a time to meet again and parted.

The commander went on ahead to his home in Nanyang. Li reported the situation to his superior, an important official attending the emperor, and asked permission to travel to the commander's home. "This is a wonderful thing!" said Li's superior. "I shall petition the emperor for you." Li and his wife received the emperor's permission to make the journey in the imperial stagecoach, with all expenses paid.

When Superintendent Li arrived in Nanyang, he found a crowd of officials to welcome him at the roadside. They all went to the home of the commander, where a great banquet awaited them. Li presented a variety of precious things to the commander and to that officer's wife, concubines, and servants. Then the commander ordered his two sons to come forward.

Although the boys were quite different in manner, they were dressed alike and no one could tell which was Li's son. Li questioned the commander about the boys, but he answered, "Recognize your son yourself." Li examined both for a long while. Then, inspired by his natural feelings, he embraced one of them and said, "This is my son!"

"And so it is!" said the commander.

Father and son held one another and wept. All who witnessed the reunion were deeply moved. They raised their cups in congratulation, and when the banquet ended, everyone had drunk to the full.

The next day the commander met with Superintendent Li. "I have already given you your son," said the commander. "How can I keep son and mother apart? I offer you the mother as well." Li's joy knew no bounds. He returned to the capital and took his son to meet his superior, who said, "He is a fine lad," and took the boy to an audience with the emperor himself.

Li's son was enrolled in the emperor's guard and later rose to be an official of the third rank, like his father.

Generally it is fortune that decides whether a man has a son; his own effort cannot make any difference. But this fortune teller was a genius in his work.

—T'ao Tsung-i

 # A Dead Son

A man of Wei named Tung Men-wu did not grieve when his son died. "You loved your son as no other father has in the world," said his wife. "Now he has died, but you do not grieve. Why?"

"There was a time," replied Tung Men-wu, "when I had never had a son. I did not grieve then. Now that he is dead, it is the same as when I had no son. What have I to grieve for?"

—Lieh Tzu

The Golden Toothpick

Mubala the Turk, who had the Chinese name Hsi-ying, was a huge hulk of a man. One day he was dining with his wife. She had speared a tasty morsel of meat with a golden toothpick and was about to place it in her mouth when a visitor came to the door. Hsi-ying went to receive the guest, and his wife, not having time to finish the bite, set it aside in a dish before getting up to prepare tea. When she returned to her place, the golden toothpick was nowhere to be found.

A young serving maid was nearby attending to her duties, and the wife suspected her of taking the toothpick. The mistress questioned the maid long and brutally until the girl, having admitted nothing, finally died of her injuries.

More than a year later a carpenter was called in to repair the roof. As he swept some dirt from the tiles, something fell to the ground and clinked lightly on the stones. It turned out to be the missing golden toothpick, together with a piece of rotted bone. They reasoned that it must have been snatched and carried to the roof by their cat, unnoticed by the maid, who carried the injustice to her grave.

How often things like this happen! So I have written the story down as a reminder for the future.

—*T'ao Tsung-i*

The King's Favorite

In ancient times the beautiful woman Mi Tzu-hsia was the favorite of the lord of Wei. Now, according to the law of Wei, anyone who rode in the king's carriage without permission would be punished by amputation of the foot. When Mi Tzu-hsia's mother fell ill, someone brought the news to her in the middle of the night. So she took the king's carriage and went out, and the king only praised her for it. "Such filial devotion!" he said. "For her mother's sake she risked the punishment of amputation!"

Another day she was dallying with the lord of Wei in the fruit garden. She took a peach, which she found so sweet that instead of finishing it she handed it to the lord to taste. "How she loves me," said the lord of Wei, "forgetting the pleasure of her own taste to share with me!"

But when Mi Tzu-hsia's beauty began to fade, the king's affection cooled. And when she offended the king, he said, "Didn't she once take my carriage without permission? And didn't she once give me a peach that she had already chewed on?"

—*Han Fei Tzu*

The Divided Daughter

In A.D. 692, the third year of the reign of the Empress Wu, the scholar Chang Yi took up residence in Hengchou, Hunan, to serve as an official there. He was a simple, quiet man with few close friends. He had fathered two daughters (no son), of which the elder had died early. The younger, Ch'ien Niang, was a beauty beyond compare.

Now, Chang Yi had a nephew named Wang Chou, who was clever and handsome. Chang Yi always thought of the boy as having a promising future, and he would say, "When the time comes, Ch'ien Niang should be his wife."

After Wang Chou and Ch'ien Niang reached maturity, they often pictured one another in their secret dreams. But neither of the families knew anything about it, and some time later when an eligible member of Chang Yi's staff sought Ch'ien Niang's hand, the father said yes.

The news made Ch'ien Niang terribly sad, and Wang Chou was bitterly disappointed. On the pretext that he was to be transferred, he requested permission to go away to the capital. Nothing could dissuade him, and so he was sent off with many gifts.

Wounded by sorrow, Wang Chou bid a final farewell and boarded the boat. By sunset he had gone several miles into the surrounding hills. That night he was lying awake when suddenly he heard the sound of footsteps along the shore. In moments the pattering reached the boat, and Wang Chou discovered that it was Ch'ien Niang, who had been running barefoot.

Wang Chou nearly went mad with delight and amazement. Gripping her hands, he asked where she had come from. She said tearfully, "Your depth of feeling moved us both in our dreams. Now they want to deprive me of my free will. I know your love will never change, and I would give up my life to repay you, so I ran away."

This was more than Wang Chou had ever expected. He could not control his excitement. He hid Ch'ien Niang in the boat, and they fled at once, pressing the journey day and night. A few months later they reached Szechwan in the far west.

Five years passed. Ch'ien Niang bore two sons. She exchanged no letters with her parents, but she thought of them incessantly. One day she said in tears to Wang Chou, "Time was when I could not desert you, so I set aside a great duty to run away to you. Now it has been five years. I am cut off from my parents' love and kindness. How am I to hold up my head in this wide world?"

Wang Chou took pity on her and said, "Let's go home; no sense in grieving like this." And so they returned together to Hengchou. When they arrived, Wang Chou went alone first to the house of Chang Yi to confess the whole affair. But Chang Yi said, "What kind of crazy talk is this? My daughter has been lying ill in her room for many years."

"But she's in my boat right now," said Wang Chou.

Amazed, Chang Yi sent someone to see if it were true. Indeed Ch'ien Niang was there, with joy on her face and spirit in her expression. The astonished servant rushed back to tell Chang Yi.

When the sick girl in the chamber heard the news, she rose and joyfully put on her jewelry, powdered her face, and dressed in her finest clothes. Then, smiling but not speaking, she went out to welcome the woman from the boat. As they met their two bodies stepped into each other and became one, fitting together perfectly. Yet there was a double suit of clothes on the single body.

The family kept the entire affair secret in the belief that it was abnormal. Only a few relatives learned the facts. Husband and wife died forty years later, and their two sons both attained the second-highest official degree and rose to be deputy commandants.

I often heard this story when I was young. There are many

different versions, and some people say it is not true. But more than eighty years after the events, I chanced to meet a magistrate of Lai Wu. His father was cousin to Chang Yi, and since this magistrate's account is the fullest I know, I have put it down on paper.

—*Ch'en Hsüan-yu*

GHOSTS
AND SOULS

✾ The Scholar's Concubine

In Paoting there was a scholar who had bought himself a literary degree and was now ready to buy a position as county magistrate. But no sooner had he packed his baggage to go to the capital for this purpose than he fell ill and could not get up for over a month. One day an unexpected caller was announced, and the sick man felt such a strange shiver of anticipation that he forgot his ailment and rushed to greet the guest. His visitor was elaborately dressed and appeared to be a man of standing. He entered making three salutations and, when asked where he had come from, replied, "I am Kung-sun Hsia, a retainer of the eleventh imperial prince. I heard that you were getting your gear ready to go to try for a position as county magistrate. If such is your intention, perhaps you would find a governor's post even more attractive?"

Not daring to be forward, the scholar declined, though he left the subject open by adding, "My sum is small, and I cannot indulge my hopes." The visitor offered to try to obtain the position if the scholar would put up half the sum and agree to pay the remainder from his profits in office. Delighted, the scholar asked the guest to explain his scheme.

"The governor-general and the governor are my closest friends," the visitor said. "For the time being, five thousand strings of cash should ensure their support. At the moment there is a vacancy in Chenting. It would be worth making a serious bid for that post."

The scholar protested that since the office was in his home province, accepting it would violate the dynasty's rule against a man's serving in his native district. But the visitor laughed cynically and said, "Don't be so pedantic. As long as you have the cash at hand, you can get across the barriers." The scholar remained hesitant, however, for the entire scheme sounded far-fetched. Then the visitor said, "There's no need for you to have doubts. Let me tell you the whole truth: This is a vacancy in the office of the city god. Your mortal hours are at an end, and you have already been entered into the registry of the dead. But if you will utilize the means available, you may still attain high station in the world of the shades." With that the visitor rose and bid the man goodbye. "Think it over for now. I shall meet with you again in three days." Then he mounted his horse and left.

Suddenly the scholar opened his eyes from what had appeared to his attendants to be a deep sleep. He said his last farewell to his wife and sons and ordered them to bring out his hoard of cash to buy ten thousand paper ingots. This depleted the entire county's supply. The ingots were piled up and mixed with paper figures of horses and attendants. Then, according to custom, they were burned day and night so that they would accrue to their owner's account in the world beyond. The final heap of ashes practically formed a mountain.

As expected, the visitor reappeared on the third day. The scholar produced his payment, and the visitor led him to an administrative office where a high official was seated in a great hall. The scholar prostrated himself. The official merely glanced at his name and, with a warning to be "honest and cautious," approved him. Next this dignitary took a certificate, summoned the scholar to the bench, and handed it to him. The scholar kowtowed, and the thing was done.

Afterwards it occurred to the scholar that as a holder of the lowest literary degree he lacked prestige, and that he needed the pomp and splendor of carriage and apparel to command the respect of his subordinates. So he purchased a carriage and horses and sent an attendant-ghost in a gorgeous carriage to fetch his favorite concubine.

When all was ready Chenting's official insignia and regalia arrived, together with an entourage that stretched half a mile along
the road—a most satisfying display. Suddenly the heralds' announcing gong fell silent and their banners toppled. Between
panic and confusion the scholar saw the horsemen dismount and
to a man prostrate themselves on the road. The men shrank to
the height of a foot, the horses to the size of wildcats! The scholar's driver cried out in alarm, "The Divine Lord Kuan has arrived!"

The scholar was terrified. He climbed down from his carriage
and pressed himself to the ground with the others. In the distance
he saw the great general of ancient times, celebrated for his fierce
justice. The Divine Lord was accompanied by four or five horsemen, their reins loosely in hand. With his whiskers surrounding
his jaws, Lord Kuan was quite unlike the world's common images
of him. But his spiritual presence was overwhelming and ferocious, and his eyes were so wide-set that they seemed almost to
touch his ears. From horseback he said, "What official is this?"

"Governor of Chenting," came the reply.

"For this piddling position," said Lord Kuan, "is such a display really needed?"

The scholar shivered, his body hairs standing on end. All at once he watched his own body contract until he became small as a boy of six or seven. Lord Kuan commanded him to arise and walk behind his horse. A temple stood at the roadside. Lord Kuan went in, faced southward in the direction of sovereignty, and ordered brush and paper so that the scholar could write down his name and native place. The new governor wrote what was asked and submitted the paper. Lord Kuan glanced at it and said in great anger, "These letters are miswritten and misshapen. The fellow is no more than a speculator, a shark loose in the official hierarchy. How could he govern the people?"

Lord Kuan then sent for the scholar's record of personal conduct. Someone at the side kneeled and presented a statement to Lord Kuan. The Divine Lord's face grew darker and fiercer than ever. Then Lord Kuan said harshly, "This cannot be allowed. On the other hand, the crime of buying office is yet smaller than the crime of selling it!" Thereupon an arresting officer in golden armor was seen leaving with ropes and collar.

Then two attendants took hold of the scholar, pulled off his official's cap and robes, and applied fifty strokes of the rod. When they expelled him through the gates, the flesh was practically torn from his backside.

The scholar peered in all directions, but there was no sign of his horse and carriage. He could not walk for pain and lay down on the grass to rest. When he raised his head and looked around, he saw that he was not too far from home. Luckily his body was light as a leaf, and within a day and a night he reached his house. The truth of it all dawned on him as he awoke from the dream and lay moaning on his bed.

The members of the family gathered to question him, but all the scholar told them was that his buttocks were sore. It seems he had lost consciousness and was virtually a dead man for seven days. Looking at the assembled household, the scholar said, "Why is my beloved Ah Lien not here?" For Ah Lien was his favorite concubine.

They told him that Ah Lien had been sitting and chatting the previous night when she suddenly said, "He has become governor of Chenting and has sent a messenger to receive me." Whereupon she went into her room, made herself up, and died.

The scholar pounded his chest in bitter remorse. Hoping that she could be revived, he ordered the corpse held and not buried. But after several days there was no sign of life, and they put her in the tomb. The scholar's illness gradually passed, but the bruises on his backside were so severe that they took six months to heal.

Time and again the scholar said to himself, "The sum I had saved to purchase office is gone, and wasted at that, and I have been the victim of punishment by the forces below. Still, I could endure it. But not to know where my beloved Ah Lien has been taken is too much to bear in the cold, quiet night."

—*P'u Sung-ling*

Three Former Lives

The scholar Liu, who won his advanced degree the same year as my elder brother, was able to recall events from his previous lives and often described them in great detail. In his first lifetime he was a member of the nobility and as corrupt as any of them. He died at the age of sixty-two and was received by the king of the dead. The king treated him as a village elder, granting him a seat and offering him tea. He noted that the tea in the king's drinking cup was clear and pure, while the tea in his own was thick and sticky. "This must be what I have to drink to be reborn with no memory of my past life," he thought. When the king was momentarily distracted, he threw the contents of his cup around the corner of the table and pretended that he had drunk the tea.

After a while the king looked up Mr. Liu's record of misdeeds in life and angrily ordered a group of ghosts to remove him. The king punished him by reincarnation as a horse, and some fierce ghosts marched him off. He found himself before a house with a threshold too high for him to cross. He balked, but the ghosts lashed him. In great pain he stumbled forward. Then he was in a stable and heard a voice saying, "The black mare has given birth to a colt. A male!" He understood the words but could not speak. Too hungry to do anything else, he went to the mare and suckled.

Four or five years went by, and his body grew strong and tall. He had a terrible fear of the whip and would shy whenever he saw it. The master always protected his body with a saddle pad and held the reins loosely, sparing him discomfort, but the groom and the servants rode him without a pad and dug their heels into his flesh so that the pain pierced him. Out of sheer indignation he refused food for three days and died.

When he came to the nether world, the king of the dead verified that his term of punishment had not expired and took him to task for evading it. The king had his hide peeled off and sent him back into the world as a dog. He was too dejected to move until the horde of ghosts lashed him savagely. In severe pain he scurried into the wilderness, thinking he would prefer death. He jumped a precipice, fell upside down, and could not get up. When he came to consciousness, he was in a dog hole. A bitch was licking him with loving care, and he realized that he had been born again into the mortal world.

As he grew into a young dog, excrement and urine seemed fragrant to him, but he knew that they were filthy and made up his mind not to eat any. He spent a year as a dog in a state of constant fury, wanting only to die. Yet he was afraid to escape this life. Since the master fed him well and showed no wish to slaughter him for food, he purposely bit him in the leg, tearing the flesh; and the master clubbed him to death.

This rash deed angered the king of the dead, and he ordered Mr. Liu whipped with hundreds of strokes. Then he turned him into a snake and confined him to a secluded room so dark that he never saw the sky. Frustrated, Mr. Liu scaled a wall and escaped through a hole. He looked at himself and found that he was on his belly in the lush grass—strange but true, a snake!

He swore that he would harm no living thing but would satisfy his hunger with fruits and vegetables. For more than a year he lived in this way, pining to kill himself but understanding that it would be unwise, just as it would be unwise for him to injure someone and get himself killed. He could not find a suitable way to die. One day as he was lying in the grass, he heard a carriage coming and rushed into the road in front of it. The wheels crushed him and cut him in two.

His speedy return amazed the king of the dead. The snake lay prostrate and told his story. The king, because the creature had been innocent when killed, forgave him and judged that he had fulfilled his sentence and could be reborn human. And so he became the scholar Liu who begins our story.

When Mr. Liu was born, he could speak. He could recite literary works, essays, and histories after only one reading, and soon he earned his advanced degree. Yet he was always urging people to put a thick pad under their horse's saddle, for a heel dug into the flank is worse punishment for a horse than the whip.

The Recorder of Things Strange says: Creatures with fur or horns include princes and lords. This is so, just as there are things furred or horned among princes and lords. For the lowly to do good deeds is like planting a tree to produce flowers. For the noble to do good deeds is like nourishing a tree that has already blossomed. What is planted should grow larger; what is nourished should last long. Otherwise, one hauls the salt wagon and suffers the fetters as a horse, or feeds on filth only to be cut up and cooked as a dog, or, clad in scales, dies in the claws of crane or stork as a snake.

—P'u Sung-ling

ஓ The Monk from Everclear

Having led a life of lofty purity, a certain monk from Everclear in Shantung province was still hale at the age of eighty. But one day he fell over and did not rise. Although the monks of the temple rushed to his aid, he had already passed into the world beyond.

The monk himself, unaware that he was dead, floated away with his soul intact until he reached the faraway borders of Honan province. In Honan at that moment, a young man of the upper classes was leading a team of horsemen who were using hawks to hunt for hares. His horse bolted, and the young man fell off and died. By chance his soul encountered that of the old monk, and the two joined as one.

After a while the young man gradually recovered consciousness. His servants surrounded him solicitously as he opened his eyes and asked, "How did I get here?" They helped him home, where an assembly of beautiful women greeted him with expressions of concern. "I am a monk!" he cried. "What am I doing here?" The members of the household thought he had lost his mind and earnestly tried to make him understand that he had been in an accident. The monk made no further attempt to explain himself; he simply shut his eyes and would not speak again.

They fed him husked rice, which he took; but he refused both wine and meat. At night he slept alone and would not accept the services of wife or concubine. After a few days he thought of going for a short walk. Everyone was delighted. He stepped out, but when he paused for a moment, a stream of attendants ap-

proached him with financial accounts to check over. He refused
to deal with these matters, claiming that he was still too weak
from his illness. All he said was, "In Shantung there is an Everclear county. Do you know of it?" The attendants replied that
they did, and he said, "I feel depressed and at a loss for anything
to do. It would please me to go there for a visit; let's get ready
now." His servants said that he had just recovered and was not
well enough for a long trip, but he would not listen.

The next day he set out. When he arrived in Everclear, the
place was as he remembered it. Without asking the way he went
directly to the monastery, and the disciples greeted their distin-
guished guest with deference. "Where has your old monk gone
to?" he asked. They replied, "Our master has gone the way of all
things." The visitor asked where the grave was, and the puzzled

disciples led him to a solitary three-foot mound not yet over-grown with wild grass.

Soon the young man mounted his horse for the return journey. "Your master was a monk of discipline, and the order that he established here should not be disturbed," he told them. The monks nodded continuously as he left.

Back in his household, the young man's mind went dead as ash. He sat in meditation like a withered tree, refusing to attend to any family responsibilities. And after several months he walked out of the house and disappeared.

He returned to the old monastery and said to the disciples, "I am none other than your master." Thinking him demented, the monks looked at one another and laughed. But when he told them the circumstances of his return to life, and when he spoke of events during the old monk's lifetime, everything tallied. The monks believed him and installed him in his former quarters, serving him as they always had.

The young man's family discovered where he was and often sent horse and carriage to the monastery with an earnest appeal for him to come home. He paid no attention to them. After a year his wife sent his steward to the monastery with many gifts, but he refused all the gold and silk and accepted only a single cloth robe. Friends who came to the district called on him to pay their respects and found him reticent and wise for his years. Though he was only thirty, he could vividly describe the events of eight decades.

The Recorder of Things Strange says: When a man dies, his spirit disperses. If a spirit should travel a thousand leagues and still remain whole, it is because that soul's nature is unalterable.It is not astonishing that such a strong-minded monk should come back to life; it is more surprising that on entering a state of magnificent luxury, he was still able to sever his ties and turn from the world. How different from those ordinary men who fall in the twinkling of an eye and stain their moral record so deeply that they'd be better off dead!

—*P'u Sung-ling*

෯ The Monk's Sins

When a man named Chang died suddenly, an underworld officer took him down to see the king of the dead. The king checked the records and was angry to learn that the officer had made a false arrest. He ordered the ghost to take Chang back to the living.

When Chang was released, he persuaded the ghost to let him see the prisons of hell. The ghost led him through the Nine Abysses, the Hill of Knives, and the Sword Trees, pointing out each thing of note. Toward the end of the tour they came to a place where a monk was hanging head down, legs bound and laced with ropes. The monk howled with pain, as if he were about to die. As he drew closer Chang saw that it was his own elder brother. Horrified and anguished, Chang asked the ghost what crimes the monk was suffering for.

"This one was a Buddhist monk," said the ghost. "He was taking money from all sides to pay for women and gambling. That's why we've punished him. We won't let him down till he repents."

Then Chang came back to life and began to wonder if his brother had already died. To find out, he hurried to his brother's home in the Temple of Blessings. He entered the gates and heard howls of pain. In one of the rooms he found his brother, whose legs, covered with welts, were propped against a wall and oozing blood and pus. Chang asked his brother why he kept his legs in that position.

"For relief," replied the monk. "Otherwise the pain goes right through me." Then Chang told him what he had seen in the world of the dead. The monk was terrified and not only abandoned his major vices but even forswore meat and wine. He recited sutras and mantras with great reverence. Within two weeks he was well again and thereafter became a model of self-discipline.

The Recorder of Things Strange says: Hell, or the dungeons of the dead, is a myth, never verified. At least, men of vicious character justify themselves by saying that there is no punishment for our misdeeds. What they fail to understand is that the disasters which strike us in our own daylight world are the punishment of the Unseen.

—*P'u Sung-ling*

The Truth About Ghosts

Ch'en Tsai-heng of my city was sixty years old, a gentle, genial, and humorous man. He was walking at day's end on the outskirts of the city when he saw two men carrying a fire in a lantern. He tried to light his pipe from the fire but could not manage it. One of the men said to him, "Have you passed your first 'post mortem' week yet?" Amazed, Ch'en replied simply, "Not yet."

"That explains it," the man said. "Your 'sun-time spirits' are not yet used up, so the 'shade-time' fire won't give you a light."

Realizing that he was speaking with the dead, Ch'en pretended to be one also. "The world claims that men fear ghosts; is that true?" he asked them.

"Not at all," replied one of the ghosts. "The truth is that ghosts fear men."

"What is it about men that could frighten a ghost?" asked Ch'en.

"Saliva."

At once Ch'en took a deep breath and spat at them. The two ghosts retreated three paces. Glaring, they said angrily, "Then you are not a ghost!"

Ch'en laughed. "In fact, not to deceive you, I am a man who is near to a ghost—near enough to spit on you." This he did again, and each ghost contracted to half its former size. He spat a third time and they vanished.

—Huang Chün-tsai

ᘒ Sung Ting-po
Catches a Ghost

When Sung Ting-po of Nanyang was walking one night, he ran across a dead soul. "Who are you?" he asked.

"A ghost," it replied, and added, "Who are you?"

"A ghost, too," said Sung Ting-po to mislead it.

"Where are you headed?" asked the ghost.

"Yüan market town."

"So am I."

And so they proceeded. After several miles the ghost said, "We have quite a way to go. How about taking turns carrying each other?"

"Fine," answered Sung Ting-po.

To begin with, the ghost carried Sung Ting-po on his shoulders for several miles. "You are so heavy, good friend," the ghost commented, "that I'm wondering if you really *are* a ghost."

"I'm a new ghost," replied Sung Ting-po, "so my body is still heavy." And Sung Ting-po took his turn carrying the ghost, which was practically weightless. They went on this way exchanging places a number of times.

"I'm a new ghost," Sung Ting-po remarked again, "so I'm not familiar with what ghosts fear and avoid."

"Human saliva," replied the ghost. And the two continued on their way. Soon they came to a stream that they had to cross, and Sung Ting-po asked the ghost to go first. It waded in and made no sound. But when Sung Ting-po followed, his body swished through the water, and the ghost asked, "How come you're making that racket?"

"It's just that the newly dead aren't used to crossing water. Don't hold it against me."

The two were approaching their destination, and it was Sung Ting-po's turn to carry the ghost. He set it upon his shoulders and then suddenly tightened his grip. The ghost cried, "Hey! Hey!" as it struggled to get down. But Sung Ting-po held fast. He marched straight into the Yüan market, and there he set it down. As the ghost touched the ground it turned into a sheep, which Sung put up for sale. Fearing that it might change itself again, he spat on it. He got 1,500 coppers for the sheep and went on his way.

This is a true story: a chronicle of the time says, "Sung Ting-po sold a ghost for 1,500 coppers."

—*Kan Pao*

The Man Who Couldn't Catch a Ghost

My father heard this story from his grandfather.

In the city of Ching there was a man named Ch'iang San-mang. He was bold and direct, with no subtlety to him. One day he heard a man tell how Sung Ting-po had caught a ghost, and how the ghost had turned itself into a sheep to escape, and how Sung Ting-po had sold it and spat on it to prevent it from changing again.

Ch'iang San-mang was overjoyed. "Now I'm sure that ghosts can be captured," he said. "If I could get one every night and turn it into a sheep, then the next morning I could bring it to the butcher's and supply myself with meat and drink for the day."

Every night thereafter he shouldered a club and, rope in hand, crept among the graves like a hunter stalking a rabbit. But he never came across anything. Places that everyone called haunted turned out to be barren, though once he even pretended to be in a drunken sleep to dare the ghosts to do their worst.

One evening he saw a few flares across the forest and rushed to the spot, but the lights dispersed like so many sparks before he arrived. After a month of this frustration, he gave up.

It would seem that the dead frighten men simply by exploiting their fear. Ch'iang San-mang was convinced that a ghost could be caught and tied up, and his fearlessness was enough to scare them off.

—*Chi Yün*

Ai Tzu and the Temple Ghost

Ai Tzu was traveling by water, and on his way he saw a temple. The temple was low and small, but it had a dignity that was impressive. In front of it ran a little ditch. As Ai Tzu watched, a man who was on foot reached the ditch but could not get across. So the man looked into the temple, grabbed a statue of the temple god, and placed it over the ditch. Then he stepped on the statue and went his way.

Another man came, saw the statue, and sighed, "Oh! for the holy image to be treated with such disrespect!" He righted the statue, rubbed it clean with his clothes, and set it reverently back in place. He bowed three times and went his way.

Moments later, Ai Tzu heard a little ghost in the temple speaking to the statue. "My Lord, you reside here as a god. You enjoy the offerings and rites of the villagers. Now this brute has insulted you; shouldn't you bring disaster down on him to teach him a lesson?"

"If there are to be any disasters," the temple god answered, "they will descend upon the second man."

"The first man walked on you; what greater insult is there?" said the small ghost. "Yet you will not ruin him. The second man showed respect for you, my Lord, and yet you want to ruin him. Why?"

"The first man," said the temple god, "no longer has faith, and I can no longer ruin him."

"True it is," said Ai Tzu, "that the gods fear the wicked."

—Attributed to Su Shih

🌸 Escaping Ghosts

Legend has it that many spooks and apparitions have plagued passersby near High Top Bridge in Hangchow. Once a solitary traveler was caught by a rainstorm there. Suddenly, convinced that the traveler was a ghost, another man under an umbrella charged toward him and forced the traveler off the bridge and into the water. Then the man fled until, seeing a light in the bathhouse east of the bridge, he hurried in for shelter.

Afterward the traveler arrived, also drenched. Panting, he said, "A ghost carrying an umbrella forced me into the river, and I nearly drowned." "I saw the same ghost!" the first man said. Eyeing one another, the two slowly realized their mistake.

On another night of storm and drizzle, a man who had no lamp was crossing the bridge when he heard the sound of clogs behind him. Turning, he saw a large head on a body some two feet tall. He stopped to gape; the head also stopped. When he went on, the head went on. When he ran, the head ran. Panicking, the man flew to the bathhouse and pushed open the door. But before he could close it again, the head entered.

Faint from terror, the man lifted candle and saw a boy wearing a pot against the rain. Because he was afraid of ghosts, the child had followed the man for protection.

—Lang Ying

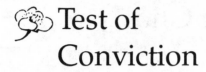 Test of
Conviction

Shih Hsü, an important general in Kiangsi, was a man skilled in
logical reasoning. One of his students also held rational views and
had always expressed the conviction that ghosts do not exist.

One day the student had an unexpected visitor, who was
dressed in black clothes with white lapels. Their conversation
touched on many subjects and eventually turned to ghosts about
which the student and the stranger
held contrary opinions. After a day
of arguing, the visitor, having been
bested, said, "Good sir,

you are more than clever with words, but your reasoning is not perfect. For I myself am a ghost! Now how can you argue that there are none?"

"Why have you come?" asked the student.

"I have been assigned to take you. Your time expires tomorrow at dinner time."

When the student pleaded in distress, the ghost said, "Do you know anyone who resembles you?"

"Yes, in Shih Hsü's command there's an officer who resembles me."

The ghost and the student went together to visit the officer. They sat down opposite him. Then the ghost took an iron pick about a foot long, set the point on the top of the officer's head, and began to pound it with a hammer.

"I feel some pain in my head," said the officer. Soon the pain became severe, and within an hour the officer was dead.

—*Kan Pao*

Drinking Companions

A fisherman named Hsü made his home outside the north gate of Tzu, a township in present-day Shantung. Every night he took along some wine to the riverside to drink while he fished. And each time, he poured a little offering on the ground "so that the spirits of those who have drowned in the river may have some wine too." When other fishermen had caught nothing, Hsü usually went home with a basketful.

One evening as Hsü was tippling by himself, a young man approached him and paced back and forth. Hsü offered him a drink and grandly shared his winejar. It was a disappointing night, however, for he failed to catch a single fish. "Let me go downstream and drive them up for you," said the young man, who rose and departed in a manner that seemed to be airborne. He returned shortly and said, "A number of fish will be arriving." And indeed, Hsü could hear a chorus of splashing as the approaching fish struck at insects. He took up his net and got several, each a foot long.

Delighted, Hsü thanked the young man and started home. Then he turned to offer his benefactor some fish, but the young man declined, saying, "I have often enjoyed your delicious brew. For my trifling assistance it's not worth speaking of reciprocity. In fact, if you wouldn't refuse my company, I'd like to make a custom of it."

"We have spent only an evening together," answered Hsü. "What do you mean by 'often enjoyed'? But it would be a pleas-

ure if you kept visiting me, though I'm afraid I don't have anything to repay your kindness." Then he asked the young man his
name.

"I am a Wang," was the reply, "but have no given name. You
could call me 'Liu-lang,' or 'Sixth-born,' when we meet." And
thus they parted.

Next day Hsü sold his fish and bought more wine. In the evening the young man was already there when Hsü arrived at the
riverbank, so they had the pleasure of drinking together again.
And again after several rounds the young man suddenly whisked
away to drive the fish for Hsü.

Things went on agreeably like this for half a year when out of
the blue Liu-lang announced to Hsü, "Ever since I had the honor
of your acquaintance, we have been closer than closest kin. But
the day of parting has come." His voice was filled with sadness.

Hsü was surprised and asked why. The young man started to
speak and then stopped several times until he said at last, "Close
as we are, the reason may shock you. But now that we are to part,
there's no harm in telling you the plain truth: I'm a ghost, one
with a weakness for wine. I died by drowning when I was drunk,
and I have been here for several years. The reason you always
caught more fish than anyone else is that I was secretly driving
them toward you in thanks for your libations. But tomorrow my
term of karma ends, and a replacement for me will be coming.
I'm to be reborn into another life on earth. This evening is all that
remains for us to share, and it is hard not to feel sad."

Hsü was frightened at first, but they had been close friends for
so long that his fear abated. He sighed deeply over the news,
poured a drink, and said, "Liu-lang, drink this up and don't despair. If our ways must part, that's reason enough for regret; but
if your karmic lot is fulfilled and your term of suffering relieved,
that's cause for congratulation, not sorrow." And together they
shared a deep swig of wine. "Who will replace you?" asked Hsü.

"You'll see from the riverbank. At high noon a woman will
drown as she crosses the river. That will be the one!" As the
roosters in the hamlet called forth the dawn, the two drinkers
parted, shedding tears.

The next day Hsü watched expectantly from the edge of the
river. A woman came carrying a baby in her arms. As she reached
the river, she fell. She tossed the child to shore, then began crying
and flailing her hands and feet. She surfaced and sank several

times until she pulled herself out, streaming water. Then she rested a little while, took her child in her arms, and left.

When the woman was sinking, Hsü could not bear it and wished he could rush to her rescue. He held back only because he remembered that she was to replace Liu-lang. But when the woman got herself out he began to doubt what Liu-lang had told him.

At dusk Hsü went fishing in the usual spot. Again his friend came and said to him, "Now we are together again and need not speak of parting for the time being." When Hsü asked why, Liu-lang replied, "The woman had already taken my place, but I had pity for the child in her arms. Two should not be lost for one, and so I spared them. When I will be replaced is not known, and so it seems that the brotherhood between us shall continue."

Hsü sighed with deep feeling. "Such a humane heart should be seen by the Highest in Heaven." And so they had the pleasure of each other's company as before.

Several days later, however, Liu-lang came to say goodbye again. Hsü thought he had found another replacement, but Liu-lang said, "No, my compassionate thought for the drowning woman actually reached to heaven, and I have been rewarded with a position as local deity in Wu township of Chauyüan county. I assume office tomorrow. Please remember our friendship and visit me; don't worry about the length or difficulty of the journey."

"What a comfort to have someone as upright as you for a deity," said Hsü, offering his congratulations. "But no road connects men and gods. Even if the distance did not daunt me, how could I manage to go?"

"Simply go; don't think about it," replied the young man. After repeating the invitation, he left.

Hsü went home to put his things in order and set out at once, though his wife mocked him. "You're going hundreds of miles? Even if this place exists, I don't think you can hold a conversation with a clay idol!" she sneered. Hsü paid no attention. He started off and eventually arrived in Chauyüan county, where he learned that there really was a Wu township. On his way there he stopped at a hostel and asked for directions to the temple. The host said with an air of pleasant surprise, "By any chance is our guest's surname Hsü?"

"Yes, how did you know?"

The host left abruptly without making a reply. Presently a mixed throng approached and circled Hsü like a wall; men carried their babies, women peeped around their doors. The crowd announced to an amazed Hsü, "Several nights ago we had a dream in which our deity said that a friend named Hsü would be coming and that we should help him out with his traveling expenses. We have been respectfully awaiting you." Marveling at this reception, Hsü went to sacrifice at the temple.

"Since we parted," he prayed, "my thoughts have dwelled on you night and day. I have come far to keep our agreement, and I am both favored and deeply moved by the sign you gave the local people. But I am embarrassed to have come without a fitting gift. All I brought was a flask of wine. If it is acceptable, let us drink as we used to on the riverbank." His prayer done, Hsü burned paper money. Shortly he saw a wind arise behind the shrine. The smoke swirled around for a time and then disappeared.

That night Liu-lang, looking altogether different now that he was capped and garbed in finery, entered Hsü's dreams. Expressing his appreciation, Liu-lang said, "For you to come so far to see me moves me to tears, but I am unable to meet you directly because I hold such a trivial position. It saddens me to be so near to the living and yet so far. The people here have some meager presents for you as a token of our past association. Whenever you are to return home, I shall see you off myself."

Hsü remained in Wu township a few more days before preparing to leave. The people of Wu tried to keep him longer, making earnest appeals and inviting him to daylong feasts with different hosts. But Hsü was set on returning home. The people outdid themselves in generosity, and before the morning passed his bags were filled with gifts. The grey-haired and the young gathered to see him out of the village. And a whirlwind followed him some three or four miles farther. Hsü bowed again and again. "Take care of yourself, Liu-lang," he said. "Don't bother coming so far. With your humane and loving heart, you can surely bring good fortune to this township without advice from old friends." The wind swirled around for a time and then was gone. The villagers, exclaiming in wonder at these events, also went to their homes.

When Hsü arrived back in his own village, his family's circumstances had improved so much that he did not return to fishing. Later he saw people from Chauyüan county who told him that the deity was working miracles and had become widely known.

The Recorder of Things Strange says: To attain the heights of ambition without forgetting the friends one made when poor and lowly—that is what made Wang Liu-lang a god! Nowadays, when do the high and noble in their carriages recognize those still wearing a bamboo hat?

—P'u Sung-ling

🌸 The Censor
and the Tiger

Li Cheng of Lunghsi in present-day Kansu was an imperial rela-
tion. As a youth he was learned and excelled in composition. At
the age of twenty he had become an esteemed and eminent
scholar and was awarded a stipend by the governor.

In the spring of the tenth year of the reign of T'ien Pao (A.D.
751) Li Cheng was one of the successful candidates under the
assistant prime minister, Yang Mo, and advanced to the highest
degree. Some·years later he was assigned to fill the vacant office
of chief constable in Chiangnan.

By nature Li Cheng was an indolent man, and arrogant because
of his talents. He could not adjust to his low position as chief
constable and felt frustrated and depressed. Whenever he met
with his colleagues, he said after a few drinks, "How could the
likes of you be in a class with me?" His associates resented this
bitterly.

In time he resigned his office and secluded himself at home for
nearly a year. Then, pressed by the necessity of earning a living,
he packed his bags and went to the southeast to seek office from
the local administrators. He had a considerable reputation in that
area, and many people gathered to study under him and enjoy his
talented company. A year or more later as he was packing to
leave, they weighed him down with generous presents.

Li was traveling home with his gifts when he stopped at a lodge
in Jufen. There he was stricken with fever and lost his senses. He
made his servant miserable and whipped him unmercifully. After

ten days the illness worsened, and Li ran raging into the night. No one knew where he had gone, though his servant waited and tried to find him. But in another month's time when Li Cheng still did not return, the servant disappeared with his master's horse and possessions.

The following year the scholar Yüan Ts'an of Ch'en prefecture was on his way to the southernmost province of Kuangtung with an imperial commission to serve as supervisory censor. He and his escort came by stagecoach to the territory of Shangyü in Honan province. As he was about to set out the next morning, the man in charge of the post station told him, "There's a tiger on the road ahead—a ferocious man-eater. No one goes through except in broad daylight. It's still too early. Stay a bit longer; you must not go ahead."

"But I am the emperor's representative," cried Ts'an angrily. "We are many on horseback, and no beast of mountain or marsh can do me harm." And he ordered the carriage forward. He had hardly gone a quarter of a mile when a tiger charged from the brush. Ts'an was terrified. Then the tiger dove for cover and spoke in a human voice, "How strange! I nearly killed my old friend!"

From the thicket Ts'an recognized the voice of Li Cheng! The two men had taken their degrees together and had been close friends, but their ways had parted years ago. Now, hearing Li Cheng's voice, Ts'an was both frightened and amazed and could not understand what was happening. Finally he asked, "Who are you? Can you be my friend Li Cheng of Lunghsi?"

The tiger moaned several times, then said to Ts'an, "I am Li Cheng. Kindly stay a few moments and have a word with me."

Ts'an got off his horse and addressed the bushes: "Dear Li Cheng, how did you come to this?"

"Since we parted long ago," said the tiger, "I have had no news of you. How have you been, and where are you bound for now? Just before, I saw two of your officers riding ahead. The courier was leading them and holding your seal of office. Can it be that you are an imperial censor on a tour of duty?"

"Recently I was fortunate to take my place as a censor. I have been sent on a mission to Kuangtung."

"You have established yourself through your literary achievements," said the tiger, "and your entering the ranks at court is truly a great fulfillment. But even greater is the integrity of the position of imperial censor, who bears the responsibility of examining the conduct of all the officials! His Majesty has exercised discretion in selecting an outstanding man like you. And it is a heartfelt satisfaction to me that you have attained this position. I greatly congratulate you."

"In times gone by," replied Ts'an, "you and I achieved recognition the same year and formed a friendship closer than the common sort. But time has raced past, while our voices have been unheard and our faces unseen by one another. My heart and eyes have been denied their hopes of seeing your excellent example. Who would have imagined that today I would hear you speak with such remembrance of our old friendship! But why are you hiding yourself instead of coming out to meet me? That's not how it should be between old friends!"

"I am no longer human," replied the tiger from the thicket. "How can I present myself to you?" Ts'an asked how such a thing could have happened, and the tiger said, "I had visited the southeast and last year was on my way home. I stopped at Jufen, where I suddenly fell ill and went mad. I raced into the hills and soon found myself walking on all fours. I could feel my heart grow ruthless, my strength enormous. My limbs had long hair on them. When I saw men in full dress on the road or rushing about with their burdens, when I saw birds aloft or animals afoot, I wanted to devour them! When I reached the south of Hanyin, I suffered the pangs of hunger. A plump man crossed my path, so I seized him and gobbled him up to the last scrap. That has become my practice ever since. Although I was an arrogant man, I still remember my family and my friends. But having violated holy sanctions, having turned suddenly into a wild beast, I have been ashamed to face anyone. Alas, you and I were awarded our degrees the same year, and we have always been close. Today you hold an imperial commission and bring honor to your parents and your friends. But I have to hide myself in the forest and abandon the world of men forever. I leap up and sigh vainly at the sky; I lower my eyes to the ground and weep. Ruined and unfit to serve—such is my fate." The tiger cried and moaned, unable to master its feelings. "If you have turned into another species, why are you still able to speak?" asked Ts'an. "It is my form that has changed," said the tiger. "My heart and mind have human understanding. But I am rude and impetuous, filled with fears and hatreds, and unable to do what is expected of a friend and host. All I ask is that you remember me and pardon my inexcusable conduct. When you return from your tour in Kuangtung, if we should meet again I shall surely forget our lifelong friendship and regard you as another meal in my trap. Be on your guard; don't let me commit such a crime and earn the scorn of my fellow scholars."

The tiger added, "You and I are as one. May I entrust something to you?"

"I would never refuse my old friend," replied Ts'an. "Please explain fully, for I am eager to help you."

"Had you not agreed," the tiger said, "I would not have dared to mention it. When I was at the inn, I fell ill and went mad. After I entered the mountains, my servant made off with my horse and baggage. My family must still be in my old village. Would they ever imagine what befell me? When you come back from the south, please send a message to them saying only that I have died—nothing of what happened today. I am in your debt if you will do this."

The tiger added, "In this world I have no property. My son is still too young to make a living for himself. You have a high position at court, and you have always set an example of morality and loyalty to friends. Nothing surpasses the friendship we had. I hope you will keep in mind how helpless my son is and see to his needs now and then, lest he perish by the roadside. What a blessing this would be!"

When he was done speaking, the tiger began to cry. Ts'an also cried and said, "We share our joys and our sorrows. Your son is as my own. I will do my utmost to comply with your grave charge. Have no worry for his welfare."

"In former times," the tiger said, "I wrote a few dozen pieces which have never circulated, and the drafts are scattered and lost. If you could transcribe them for me, while I would never dream of their being noted publicly, they may contain something useful to pass on to my descendants."

Ts'an called for a servant to bring writing materials and wrote as the tiger recited. It came to nearly twenty chapters. The style was lofty, the meaning profound. Ts'an sighed over and over as he read the text.

"These tell of the things I tried to do, the man I tried to be," said the tiger. "I have no right to expect that my words will mean anything to future generations. But you are on a mission and have a schedule to meet; if you dally here too long, the courier will fret over missing the next stage. So now our ways part for good. The sorrow this causes me cannot be described."

After a prolonged goodbye, Ts'an left. The first thing he did when he returned from the south was to dispatch a letter to Li Cheng's son with some money for the funeral. In a month's time the son came to the capital and called at Ts'an's residence to ask for his father's coffin. Having no choice, the imperial censor told him all. Later Ts'an shared his official salary with Li's wife and son to spare them any hardship. Eventually Ts'an rose to become vice minister of war.

—Chang Tu

✿ Underworld Justice

Hsi Lien of Tungan, a county in Hunan province, was a gullible, artless man and that is how he had a falling-out with the Yangs, a rich family in the same hamlet. Old Yang had died a few years before, and now Hsi Lien was at death's door. "Old Yang has bribed agents of the underworld to beat me," he cried. Hsi Lien's body became red and swollen. He moaned once and was no more.

Hsi Fang-p'ing, his son, could not eat for grief. "Father was a plain and simple man," he said, "and not clever with words. Now he has suffered injustice at the hands of a vile ghost, and I'm going to take myself to that world below and plead his cause." Those were the last words Hsi Fang-p'ing spoke for many a day. He would stand, he would sit, but he seemed to have lost his mind, for his soul had already departed from his body.

As Hsi Fang-p'ing's spirit set out on the journey, he had no idea where he was headed. But he asked his way of travelers on the road, and they directed him to the city where his father was already in prison. Hsi went to the prison gates and saw his father lying under the eaves, a wreck of his former self. When the father lifted his eyes and saw his son, he wept pathetically. "All the jailors take bribes," he said. "They have been beating me day and night. My legs are like pulp."

Hsi cursed the jailors. "If my father has committed a crime, he should be tried according to the law of the realm," he said angrily. "How can you underworld demons take the law into your own hands?" Then he went out and prepared a written complaint. He appeared at the morning sessions held by the city god, voiced his grievance, and submitted the paper. Old Yang took fright and began passing out gifts before presenting himself to answer the charges. The city god showed Hsi Fang-p'ing no consideration and held that his complaint was groundless. Furious but without recourse, Hsi traveled some ten leagues in the kingdom of the dead until he reached the governor's seat, where he complained formally about the favoritism shown by the city god and his underlings. The governor delayed judgment for half a month, then had Hsi beaten and ordered the city god to repeat the trial.

Hsi arrived at the city again and was placed in the stocks, where he fumed because he could not make his wrongs known. Fearing that Hsi would try to appeal further, the city god sent guards to escort him forcibly home to the world of the living. The guards excused themselves at the gates to the upper world, and Hsi did not go through. He sneaked back to the underworld to appeal to the king of the dead against the cruelty and greed of the governor and the city god.

The king at once took the two officials into custody to answer the charges. So the pair secretly sent their trusted henchmen to negotiate with Hsi, offering him one thousand pieces of silver if he would drop the case. Hsi rebuffed them. Several days later the keeper of the inn where Hsi was staying said to him, "You are too proud, my friend. The officials are seeking accommodation with you, but you are resisting them. I understand that each of them has offered gifts to the king, and I fear your cause is doomed." Hsi took this to be idle rumor.

But soon the court attendants came to summon him before the king of the dead, and the king was in a fury. He would not allow Hsi to make a deposition; instead he ordered twenty strokes for him.

"What's my offense?" cried Hsi, but the king seemed to hear nothing.

"I'm only getting what I deserve!" shouted Hsi. "After all, who told me to be poor? No one; so it must be my fault."

The King grew even angrier and ordered him placed on a bed of fire. Two ghosts seized Hsi and took him away to the east yard, where there was an iron bed frame with a fire burning under it. The surface of the bed glowed red hot. The ghosts stripped him bare and heaved him onto it, kneading him and rolling him back and forth. The pain was intense. His bones and flesh were charred black, and he wished for death. After two hours of this, the ghost said, "Enough!" Then they lifted him up and told him to come down and put on his clothes. Luckily he could walk, though he was lame.

Back at the hall of justice, the king of the dead said to him, "Will you still seek a new trial?"

"A great wrong has yet to be rectified," replied Hsi. "So long as heart and mind survive in me, it would be an insult to Your Majesty for me to withdraw. I demand the trial."

"What evidence will you present?" the king asked.

"Evidence of all that I have suffered."

In a passion the king ordered his men to saw through Hsi Fang-p'ing's body. The two ghosts took him to a wooden pole eight feet high with two boards standing at the foot of the pole. The tops and bottoms of the boards were dark with bloodstains. The ghosts were about to tie him to the planks when a shout came from the hall for "someone named Hsi." The two ghosts marched him back. The king of the dead asked him, "Still brazen enough to call for a trial?"

"I demand a trial," was Hsi Fang-p'ing's answer.

The king ordered them to hurry him away and cut him open. The ghosts squeezed Hsi between the two boards and tied them to the pole. Then they began to saw. Hsi felt the top of his head slowly coming apart. Pain enveloped him, but he bore it without crying out. "Tough son of a gun," he heard a ghost comment. The saw grated as it reached Hsi's chest. "He's a devoted son, and pure in heart," he heard a ghost say. "Tilt the saw a bit so we don't damage the heart." Hsi felt the blade curving as it moved downwards. The pain doubled. His torso was divided. The boards were removed, and his two halves fell to the ground.

The ghosts ascended the hall of justice to report on their mission. They were commanded to reunite the body and present it. The ghosts pushed the halves together, rejoined Hsi, and dragged him along the street. He could feel the strain on the seam where he had been sawed, for it ached and threatened to split open again. He stumbled and fell before he could move a step. One of the ghosts took a silk ribbon from his waist and gave it to Hsi, saying, "In recognition of your filial piety." Hsi tied it on, and instantly his body felt vigorous and free of pain. He ascended the hall and prostrated himself.

There the king of the dead repeated his question. Afraid to incur further suffering, Hsi answered simply, "I shall not press the charges." The king immediately ordered him sent back to the world of the living. Escorts led him out the north gates, showed him the way home, and left. Hsi concluded that the officers of the dead were even more lawless than those in the world of the living. He could think of no way that he might reach the ear of the Highest, but he was determined to try.

It was widely held in the world that the god Erh Lang of Kuan-k'ou township in Szechuan was a relative of the Highest—of God in Heaven. Hsi Fang-p'ing decided that if he could appeal to Erh Lang, who was regarded as both astute and upright, a miracle was still possible. Glad to be free of the two escorts, Hsi turned and went south. But two men caught up with him and said, "The king guessed that you would not go home, and he was right." They bundled him back to the king of the dead.

Hsi expected the king to be angrier than ever and the consequences to be even worse. But the king's expression was not severe at all. "Your intentions are sincerely filial," he told Hsi. "I have already redressed the wrong your father suffered. By now he has been reborn into a family of wealth and status. You will not have to appeal any further. We're sending you home with one thousand pieces of silver and a guarantee that you will live to the age of one hundred years. Are you satisfied?"

The king recorded this in the registry of life and death and set his huge seal upon it. Hsi was invited to inspect the entry personally. He expressed his appreciation and withdrew. The two ghosts accompanied him, but when they reached the road they began to drive him along and curse him. "What a cunning villain you are! Making us dash all over the place until we're nearly dead! Any more trouble from you, and we'll throw you in the mill and grind you to bits."

Hsi opened his eyes wide and yelled at them, "What's this madness, you devils? You think I can endure being sawed in half but not the sting of your lashes? Let's go back to see the king. If he has ordered me home, you need not trouble yourselves to escort me." Hsi started running back the way they had come. This alarmed the ghosts, who spoke gently to him and persuaded him to resume his journey. As they went, Hsi purposely slowed his pace and rested often by the roadside, but the ghosts did not complain.

In about half a day they reached a hamlet. The ghosts sat down to rest in front of a house with a door that was slightly ajar. Hsi seated himself on the threshold, and the ghosts caught him unawares and pushed him inside the door. When he had gotten control of himself, he discovered that he had been born again an infant. He cried in indignation, refused his mother's breast, and perished in three days.

Separated from his reincarnated body, Hsi Fang-p'ing's nebulous soul wavered. Yet he did not forget about Erh Lang, the god from Kuank'ou. Hsi's soul had moved a dozen miles along the road when it was surprised by an approaching cavalcade: banners and spears blocked the way. Ducking across the highway to avoid it, he ran into the bearers of the imperial regalia and was seized by the front horsemen. They bound him and brought him before a chariot, which held a magnificent young man. "Who are you?" he asked Hsi.

Since the young man seemed to be a great minister, Hsi related his woes in detail. He ordered Hsi freed and told him to follow the chariot. Presently they arrived at a place where a dozen officials greeted them by the side of the road. The minister questioned each of them, then pointed to Hsi and told one official, "Here is a man from the world below who wishes to lodge a complaint. The matter should be resolved quickly."

Only then did Hsi learn from the entourage that the god in the chariot was the Ninth Imperial Prince of Heaven and that he had assigned Erh Lang to the case. Hsi examined Erh Lang closely. He was tall and slender and had a great beard, quite different from what the world of men pictured. After the Imperial Prince had gone, Hsi followed Erh Lang to a courthouse, where he found his father Lien, and Old Yang, together with the underlings from the kingdom of the dead.

Soon some prisoners came out of the cage-carts: the city god, the governor, and the king of the dead himself! They were interrogated then and there in each other's presence, and all Hsi Fang-p'ing's charges were confirmed. The three officials trembled in fear, cowering like rats. Erh Lang drew his pen and immediately passed sentence, and the text was shown to all the parties:

We find as follows: He who serves as king of the dead, undertaking an office of princely rank and enjoying the grace of the Highest, must have the probity and purity to lead all the officials in service, and must have no appetite for corruption. But you have used the splendor and power of your office in a vainglorious display of status. With goatish stubbornness and wolfish avarice you have sullied your integrity before the Highest.

As the axe strikes the wedge and the wedge cuts the wood, your conduct starts a chain reaction that eventually sucks the blood out of women and children. As the whale devours the fish and the fish devours the shrimp, so the life of the lowly is miserable. Let the waters of the West River be drawn to purge your innards. Let your seat of insolent luxury be consigned to flames at once. Then we shall place you in the boiling cauldron which you yourself have used to force many a victim to confess!

As for the city god and the governor, in behalf of the Highest they serve the common people as parent-officials, pastors of the human flock. Though they are offices of lower rank, a true office-seeker will not disdain them. Even if they are pressured by higher officials, they should resist. But you two brandish your hawklike claws, giving no thought to the poverty of the people. You have worked with the cunning of a monkey, indifferent to the plight of the dead. Taking bribes to pervert the law, you hid a bestial heart behind a human face! You shall have the marrow scooped from your bones and the hair plucked from your hides. You shall suffer death even in the realm of the dead and be reborn beasts, not men.

As for the underlings, since they are already demons and not of a human kind, if they will concentrate on amending their conduct in public office, they may be reborn in human form. They must not stir up waves in the sea of suffering and commit such sins as overcast the very heavens. Their lawless arrogance has brought injustices that have caused heaven to send summertime frost in sympathy. Their raging ferocity has severed man's world from the gods' and terrorized the kingdom of the dead until every man knows that he must revere only the jailor. And they have aided ignorant officials in their cruelty, making them feared as butchers. To the execution grounds with them! Chop up their limbs and boil them. Then pick from the cauldron whatever remains of muscle or bone.

And now for this fellow Yang, who though wealthy was inhumane, contentious, and full of deceit. He covered the ground with bribes, shrouding the throne of the king of the dead in darkness, creating a stench of copper cash that reached unto the heavens, robbing the realm of the dead of all justice. The corruption had spread so far that ghosts were in his employ, and his influence was felt among the gods. Yang's household shall be confiscated and given to Hsi Fang-p'ing to repay his filial conduct. Let all the prisoners now be taken to the T'ai Mountain for execution of punishment.

The god Erh Lang turned to Hsi Lien and said, "We are mindful of your son's devotion and your own gentle nature and therefore grant you a thirty-year extension among the living." Erh Lang assigned two officers to escort father and son home to their hamlet. Hsi Fang-p'ing copied the text of the decision and read it with his father on the way.

When they reached home, Hsi Fang-p'ing came to himself first. He had his father's coffin opened and the body examined. It was stiff and icy, but after a few days it gradually warmed and at last revived. Hsi searched for the copy of Erh Lang's writ, but it had vanished into the Unseen.

The Hsi household prospered. Within three years they had extended their fertile acres throughout the countryside, while the fortunes of Yang's descendants declined until their buildings and farms came into the possession of Hsi. Once a villager bought one of the Yang fields. That night he was scolded in his dreams by a god for taking what belonged to Hsi. The villager ignored the warning, but after he had planted the field and reaped less than a peck of grain, he resold the land to Hsi. Hsi Lien himself lived beyond ninety years of age.

The Recorder of Things Strange says: Everyone speaks of paradise, forgetting that the living and the dead are worlds apart, and that every sense or thought is lost in death. Not knowing whence he comes, how can man know whither he goes, much less the events of repeated deaths and rebirths? Thus how great the accomplishment of young Hsi Fang-p'ing, whose loyalty and filial love stayed firm through an eternity!

—*P'u Sung-ling*

✿ Sharp Sword

Toward the end of the Ming Dynasty the Shantung region was filled with bandits, and every township had to post soldiers for protection. Whenever a bandit was caught, he was swiftly executed. In one township called Chanch'iu there was a soldier who carried an extremely sharp sword. When he struck, it seemed as if he were drawing the blade through empty air, touching neither flesh nor bone.

It happened that ten bandits were captured and brought to the Chanch'iu authorities. One of the prisoners recognized the soldier with the sharp sword and sidled up to him. "They say your sword is so sharp it can cut off a man's head in a single stroke," he ventured. "I wonder if you would execute me."

"Very well," replied the soldier. "But take care to stay close to me. Don't get separated." The bandit followed the soldier to the execution grounds. The soldier drew his sword, flourished it, and in a flash cut the prisoner's head off. It rolled several feet and was still turning when it exclaimed admiringly, "Some sharp sword!"

—*P'u Sung-ling*

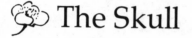 # The Skull

When Chuang Tzu was going to Ch'u he saw a hollow skull, a shape gleaming white. He stirred it with his whip and spoke, "Have you come to this, good sir, lusting for life and losing all order and reason? Was it through the overthrow of your state? Or through the executioner's axe? Was it bcause of misconduct that brought shame to your entire family? Or perhaps from hunger and cold, or simply the length of your years?"

With these words Chuang Tzu took up the skull, made himself a pillow with it, and went to sleep. During the night the skull appeared to him in a dream and said, "You spoke to me like a pedantic debater. And what you described were the heavy cares of human life, which the dead do not have. Would you like to know the meaning of death, my friend?"

Chuang Tzu said yes, and the skull continued, "The dead have no king above them and no subjects below them; neither have they the toil of the seasons. Only heaven and earth limit their span of time. Even the southward-facing sovereigns have no pleasures surpassing these." Doubtfully, Chuang Tzu said, "Suppose I were to have the fates restore your physical form—the bones, the flesh, the skin—and return you to your family, your neighbors, and your friends. Would you be willing?"

The skull seemed to frown as it said, "Do you think I would throw away the pleasures of sovereignty to go back to the wearisome world of men?"

—*Chuang Tzu*

JUDGES AND
DIPLOMATS

The Sheep Butcher and His King

King Chao of the state of Ch'u lost his country. Yüeh the sheep butcher followed the king in flight. When King Chao returned to power, he intended to reward those who had remained with him. When Yüeh's turn came, that follower said to the king's messenger, "The king lost his country. I lost my butcher shop. The king regained his country. I regained my butcher shop. Since my position and my income have been restored, is any further reward necessary?"

This was reported to the king, who said, "Make him take it."

This was reported to the sheep butcher, who said, "The king did not lose power through any fault of mine. And I never expected to suffer punishment for it. The king did not regain power through any merit of mine. So I never expected a reward for it."

This was reported to the king, who said, "Have him appear before me."

This was reported to the sheep butcher, who said, "The law of Ch'u says that no one may be presented to the king save for a great reward for great achievements. In this case I lacked the knowledge to keep the state from harm, and I lacked the courage to die resisting the traitors. When the enemy army entered the capital, I fled from the fighting out of fear, not because I was purposely following His Majesty. Now His Majesty wants to set the law aside and receive me. This is not the way for a subject to become publicly known."

The king of Ch'u said to his commander of the army, "This Yüeh, the butcher, holds a position of little esteem, yet he expounds most loftily upon the duty of a subject. Would you invite him on our behalf to become one of the three chief ministers?"

This was reported to Yüeh, who said, "I understand that such a position is far above a butcher's trade, and that a salary of ten thousand is far beyond what a sheep butcher could earn. But how could I, because of greed for office and wealth, allow my sovereign to have a reputation for absurd generosity? I do not deserve the honor. I wish to return to my trade."

Thus Yüeh declined the reward for good.

—*Chuang Tzu*

The Prime Minister's Coachman

Yen Tzu was the prime minister of Ch'i. One day when he went out, his coachman's wife watched her husband from the gates. The coachman was sheltered by a large awning befitting his rank. He laid the whip to the team of four horses, his spirits jaunty, his mood self-satisfied. But when he returned home, his wife said that she wanted to leave him. The coachman asked her reasons. "Yen Tzu is hardly five feet tall," she replied, "and he is the prime minister, renowned among the lords of the realm. I have noticed that when he goes for a drive, he seems serious and reflective and always has an air of humility. You are more than six feet tall, but you serve others as a coachman and seem very pleased with yourself. That's why I want to leave you." Thereafter the coachman made less of himself. Yen Tzu was struck by the change and asked the reason. The coachman told Yen Tzu, who promoted him.

—Ssu-ma Ch'ien

❧ The Royal Jewel

King Hui of Chao called for his adviser Lin Hsiang-ju and said, "The king of Ch'in is offering to exchange fifteen towns for the royal jewel. Should we give it up?"

"Ch'in is strong, and we are weak," replied Hsiang-ju. "We have no choice."

"What if they take the jewel and don't give us the towns?" King Hui asked.

Hsiang-ju said, "If Ch'in is offering its towns for the jewel and we refuse, we are in the wrong. If we present the jewel and they do not give the towns, they are in the wrong. Between these two possibilities, it seems better for us to have Ch'in in the wrong."

"Whom can we send?" asked the king.

"If Your Majesty has no one else, I am willing to go as your representative to present the jewel. If the towns are handed over to us, the jewel will remain with Ch'in. If the towns are not handed over, I will undertake to have the jewel restored intact."

And so King Hui of Chao sent Hsiang-ju west to deliver the jewel.

The king of Ch'in was seated upon his screened dais when he received Hsiang-ju. Hsiang-ju presented the jewel to the king, who was greatly pleased. He passed it around for his female escorts and his attendants to admire. And they all shouted, "Long live the king!"

Hsiang-ju concluded that the king of Ch'in had no intention of paying the fifteen towns for the jewel. So he stepped forward and said, "The jewel has a small flaw which I should like to point out to Your Majesty."

The king handed the jewel to Hsiang-ju, who clutched it tightly, jumped back, and steadied himself against a pillar. He was so angry that his hair seemed to be pushing up against his cap!

"If Your Majesty wants this jewel," Hsiang-ju cried, "you must send a letter to my king in Chao. He will confer with his advisers, who will all say that the state of Ch'in is so greedy that she is counting on her greater might to get our royal jewel! They will judge that your promises are empty and that you don't intend to give us the towns in exchange. And they will decide not to part with the jewel! My own humble view is that even in the relations among ordinary people there can be no dishonesty. How much more faithful should great states be to this rule!"

Hsiang-ju continued, " For us to have thwarted the pleasure of the mighty state of Ch'in would have made no sense. And so my king, after spending five days in religious abstinence, sent me to deliver the royal jewel and humbly submit a letter to your court—out of reverence for your great state's prestige and to show our respect. But when I arrived, I was received in a routine audience with little ceremony. And once you had the royal jewel, you passed it to the women around you in order to have a little amusement at my expense. I concluded that you had no intention of keeping your part of the bargain. That is why I have taken back the jewel. If Your Majesty tries to get it by force, I am going to smash my own head, together with the jewel, against this pillar."

Hsiang-ju eyed the pillar as if he were about to carry out his threat. Fearing that the jewel would be destroyed, the king of Ch'in apologized. Then he called for an official to spread out a map, on which he indicated the fifteen sites he was assigning to Chao.

Hsiang-ju judged that the king of Ch'in was only pretending to cede the towns to Chao, so he said, "The royal jewel is a world-renowned treasure. The king of Chao had to offer it to you because he was afraid of you. Before my king sent the jewel, he purified himself for five days. Your Majesty should now do the same, and then should hold the full ceremonies for a state visitor. At that time I shall present the jewel."

The king of Ch'in decided that he could not use force, so he agreed to the five days of ceremonial purification and housed Hsiang-ju in a splendid reception hall.

Hsiang-ju, however, still felt sure that the king of Ch'in would go back on his word. So he sent one of his men in plain dress back to Chao with the jewel. After the five days, the king of Ch'in

opened the state ceremonies for Hsiang-ju. But Hsiang-ju said, "Not one of the last twenty kings of Ch'in has held to his commitments. I am truly fearful that I shall be deceived and thus fail my own state. For that reason I had one of my men take the jewel back to Chao, and I expect he has arrived by now."

Hsiang-ju smiled persuasively and continued, "Ch'in is powerful and Chao is not. If Your Majesty would send a single envoy to our state, we will surrender the jewel at once. Now, if Ch'in with all its superiority will first relinquish the towns and confer them on Chao, how could we dare to retain the jewel and give offense to Your Majesty? Well I know that the crime of deceiving Your Majesty merits death, and I am willing to be thrown into the cauldron. All I ask is that Your Majesty consult with his advisers and consider my proposal fully."

The king of Ch'in looked at his advisers and scowled. His attendants wanted to take Hsiang-ju to the dungeons, but the king said, "If we kill Hsiang-ju we will never get the jewel, and the friendship between Ch'in and Chao will be broken. It would be better to treat him generously on this occasion and let him go home. I don't think the king of Chao is going to cheat us over one jewel."

The king received Hsiang-ju formally and, after a full ceremony, sent him home to Chao.

—Ssu-ma Ch'ien

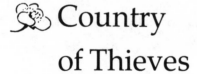 Country
of Thieves

Yen Tzu the diplomat was preparing to go on a mission to the state of Ch'u. The king of Ch'u learned of it and said to his advisers, "Yen Tzu is the state of Ch'i's shrewdest talker. When he comes, I would like to embarrass him. How can I do it?" "After he arrives," they said, "we suggest that a man in fetters be brought past Your Majesty. Let Your Majesty ask, 'What has the man done?' And we will reply, 'He's a man from Ch'i.' Then ask what his crime was, and we will say he has been convicted of theft."

When Yen Tzu arrived, the king of Ch'u toasted him until they were growing mellow with the wine. Then two officers came toward the king with a bound man. "What has he done?" asked the king. "He's from Ch'i, " they replied, "convicted of theft." The king looked at Yen Tzu and said, "Are the people of Ch'i really expert thieves?" Yen Tzu came off his mat and knelt before the king. "They say the orange tree produces a dry, sour orange when it grows in the south, a sweet, juicy one when it grows in the north. The leaves are similar, the taste of the fruit altogether different. Why so? Because the soil and water are not the same. Now, the people who are born in our northern state of Ch'i do not steal. When they go south to Ch'u they do. This can only be because the soil and water of Ch'u make them good at stealing"

—*Ssu-ma Ch'ien*

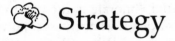 Strategy

When the army of Ch'i moved against our state of Lu, our patriarch was determined to meet them in battle. Ts'ao Kuei sought an audience with him, though Ts'ao's companions disapproved. "His counselors are working on a strategy," they said. "Why interfere?" "The counselors lack the vision for long-range planning," said Ts'ao Kuei. So he went to see the patriarch.

"What will you fight with?" he asked the patriarch, who replied, "With my loyal followers, who support me because I share the kingdom's wealth with them instead of keeping it for myself."

"Material dividends will not inspire the people to follow you," answered Ts'ao Kuei. The patriarch said, "And I have always given the gods their due, insisting on full measure in the goods that are sacrificed to them."

"Ritual will not win the favor of the gods," answered Ts'ao Kuei. The patriarch said, "I am compassionate and show mercy to all criminals, even though I cannot study every case."

"*There* is a quality that will win the loyalty of your people," answered Ts'ao Kuei. "You can win a battle with that. Please let me be your adviser at the front."

The patriarch allowed Ts'ao Kuei to share his chariot. The battle lines formed at Ch'angshuo, and the patriarch was ready to signal the advance with a drum roll. "Not yet," said Ts'ao Kuei. The enemy sounded their drums three times. "All right, sound our drums," said Ts'ao Kuei. Ch'i's army was routed.

Next the patriarch was ready to order a pursuit. "Not yet," said Ts'ao Kuei, and he got down to examine the chariot tracks of the routed army. Then he stood up on the chariot's high bar to survey the retreating enemy in the distance. "All right, pursue," he said. And they drove off the army of Ch'i.

After the victory, the patriarch asked Ts'ao Kuei for his reasoning. "In warfare," replied Ts'ao Kuei, "morale is the main thing. The first drum roll rouses the spirit of valor; at the second roll it wanes; and by the third roll it is gone. When their valor was spent, ours was at the full. That's the reason we defeated them. Now, a great power is hard to outwit. I had to be wary of an ambush, so I examined their chariot tracks and observed the disarray of their banners. When it was clear that they were truly retreating, it was time to pursue them."

—*Tso Ch'iu-ming*

🌸 Buying Loyalty

Feng Hsüan was a man of rank in the land of Ch'i, but he had fallen on such hard times that he was almost starving. In desperation he sent his attendant to Lord Meng-ch'ang, whose service Feng was seeking to enter.

"What interests your master?" asked Lord Meng-ch'ang.

"Nothing," came the reply.

"Well, what kind of work can he do?"

"None."

Amused by these replies, the easygoing nobleman agreed to accept Feng Hsüan into his household. But the lord's lieutenants assumed that their master had no respect for the newcomer and provided him with the coarsest food. After some time of this treatment, Feng Hsüan began slouching against a column of the palace and tapping it with his sword as he sang:

> O faithful sword, must we return?
> There is no fish for me to eat.

The lieutenants reported this to Lord Meng-ch'ang, who said, "Serve him the same food that you give all the members of my household."

The lord's followers did so, but after another period of time Feng Hsüan again tapped his sword as he sang:

> O faithful sword, must we return?
> There is no coach for me to ride.

The lieutenants made fun of Feng Hsüan and reported his complaint to their lord, who replied, "Prepare a horse and carriage for him as if he were a ranking member of the household."

From then on, Feng Hsüan would mount his coach, raise his sword, and ride past his companions, saying, "Now the lord treats me properly."

But after more time had passed, Feng Hsüan went back to tapping his sword as he sang:

> O faithful sword, must we return?
> I lack for means to keep my house.

Now the lieutenants viewed him with ill will as a greedy man for whom enough was not enough. But Lord Meng-ch'ang asked, "You have parents, Master Feng?"

"An elderly mother," came the reply.

And the lord sent a deputy to see to the woman's living so that she would not be in want. And Feng Hsüan never sang his song again.

It happened that Lord Meng-ch'ang took out his accounts one day and asked who in the household was skilled at bookkeeping and could collect his debts in the township of Hsüeh. Feng Hsüan wrote, "Can do" and signed his name. Lord Meng-ch'ang was puzzled, for he did not recall the man. But his lieutenants said, "It's that same fellow who used to sing the 'Faithful sword, must we return?' song." And the lord laughed and said, "Our visitor has some ability after all. I have been inattentive and failed to receive him formally."

So Feng Hsüan was called to an audience with the lord, who apologized for the delay. "I have been overworked and distracted by my concerns," he said. "Also, it is my nature to be somewhat slow and stolid. I have become so absorbed in affairs of state that I have given you offense, Master. Yet you seem to bear no grudge and, I understand, have even expressed willingness to go to Hsüeh and collect my debts."

"Yes," said Feng Hsüan and left to arrange for his transportation, put his things in order, and pack the debtors' bonds in his coach. Taking formal leave of Lord Meng-ch'ang, he asked, "When I have finished, what should I buy for you with the money?"

"See what my household has least of," replied the lord.

Feng Hsüan drove hard toward Hsüeh. When he arrived, he instructed his officers to summon all the debtors of the township to appear with their loan certificates. After each had presented his, Feng Hsüan forged Lord Meng-ch'ang's name to an order forgiving all the debts of the people, and on this authority he burned the certificates.

"Long live our lord!" the people cheered.

Feng Hsüan rode back nonstop and reached the palace in the early morning. At once he requested an audience. Marveling at his speed, Lord Meng-ch'ang put on the formal cap of office and received Feng, asking, "Are the debts collected? How did you get back so soon?"

"Collected," replied Feng Hsüan.

"And what have you acquired for me?"

"You said, 'See what my household has least of.' So I took the liberty of inspecting everything. I found that your palace is heaped with elegant treasure; your stables and kennels are well stocked; beautiful women fill the lower quarters. I judged that what your household most lacked was loyalty, and I presumed to buy some for you."

" 'Buying loyalty' means what?" asked the lord.

"My lord," Feng Hsüan replied, "you own the paltry township of Hsüeh. But far from treating the people with a father's affection, you have exploited it like a merchant. So I took the liberty of signing your name to an order forgiving the people their debts, and on that authority I burned the certificates. The people cheered. And that is how I bought their loyalty for you."

Glumly, Lord Meng-ch'ang told him, "You have said enough."

One year later a new king of Ch'i informed Lord Meng-ch'ang that his position could no longer be guaranteed. "I shall not be keeping my father's ministers as my own," said the king.

Lord Meng-ch'ang had to go back to his township of Hsüeh. He was still some twenty miles away when the people welcomed him on the road, steadying the elders and leading the children up to do him honor. Then Meng-ch'ang called Feng Hsüan to him and said, "Now I understand how you have bought loyalty for me."

—*Chan Kuo Ts'e*

The Groom's Crimes

Lord Ching, the marquis of Ch'i, assigned a groom to care for his favorite horse. But the horse died suddenly, and the lord was furious. He ordered his men to cut off the groom's limbs.

It happened that Yen Tzu was attending the lord, and when the lord's men entered, their swords at the ready, Yen Tzu stopped them. He said to Lord Ching, "In the time of the sage-kings Yao and Shun, who ruled by example only, if anyone was to be dismembered, whose limbs would they begin with?"

"With the king's own limbs," said Lord Ching. And he canceled the punishment. Instead he gave orders to have the groom condemned to death by due process.

"In that case," said Yen Tzu, "the man will die ignorant of his crimes. Shall I spell them out for him, my lord, so that he may know them before he is executed?"

"Very well," said Lord Ching.

Yen Tzu told the groom, "You have committed three crimes. You were assigned to care for the horse, and you let it die instead. That's one crime you deserve death for. Second, the horse was his lordship's favorite. That's the second reason you deserve to die. And third, you earned your fate by causing his lordship to put a man to death for the sake of a mere horse. For when the people learn of it, they will resent our lord. And when the other feudal lords learn of it, they will despise our state. So by killing his lordship's horse, you create ill feeling among the people and weaken our state in the eyes of its neighbors. Now you stand condemned to death!"

Lord Ching sighed deeply. "Set the groom free, sir, set the groom free," he cried, "lest my humanity be diminished."

—Yen Tzu Ch'un Ch'iu

🌸 The Chain

The king of Wu wanted to attack the state of Ching. He told his advisers so, adding, "Whoever dares to criticize me dies." One of the king's followers had a young son who wanted to object but was afraid to. He took a pellet and a sling and went rambling in the gardens behind the palace until the dew had soaked his clothes. For three days he continued this threshing through the shrubbery. At last the king of Wu noticed him and asked, "What's the point of getting yourself sopping wet?"

"In the garden there's a tree," answered the young man, "and perched on the tree is a cicada singing sadly, sipping the dew, unaware of the praying mantis behind him. Crouching, twisting, the mantis is trying to grab the cicada, unaware that behind it is an oriole stretching its neck to swallow the mantis. Nor does the oriole reaching out to peck know that there is a slingshot below aimed at him. All three, intent on what is in front, do not notice the danger behind."

"Well spoken," said the king of Wu. And he called off the attack on Ching.

—Liu Hsiang

 # Hearsay

Lieh Tzu was poor, and he looked terribly underfed. Someone mentioned it to the prime minister, Cheng Tzu-yang: "Lieh Tzu is a widely known scholar of the Tao. If he suffers poverty while living in your lordship's state, might not your lordship be thought hostile to scholars?"

Tzu-yang lost no time in sending an official to Lieh Tzu with a gift of food. Lieh Tzu came forth to receive the minister's messenger and bowed deeply, but he declined the gift. The messenger left. Lieh Tzu went back inside his home, where his wife smote her breast and stared at her husband in despair.

"Your humble wife always thought that the families of men of the Tao would gain ease and pleasure," she said. "Now in our direst need the prime minister sends someone to honor us with a gift of food—and you refuse it! Such is my fate!"

Lieh Tzu smiled and said to his wife, "The prime minister does not know of me for himself. He sent us food on the say-so of a third party. Should the time come to condemn me, it's all too likely to happen also on the say-so of a third party. That's the reason I refused his gift."

Eventually the common people overthrew Tzu-yang.

—*Lieh Tzu*

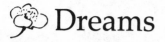 # Dreams

The head of the Yin clan in the state of Chou had vast holdings, and his servants worked without rest from dawn until dark. There was one aged servingman whose muscles were sapped of all strength, but the head of the clan only drove him all the harder. The old man groaned as he faced his tasks each day. At night he slept soundly, insensible from fatigue, his vital spirits at ebb. And each night he dreamed that he was king of the realm, presiding over all the people, taking full command of the affairs of state. He feasted carefree in the palace, and every wish was gratified. His pleasure was boundless. But every morning he awoke and went back to work.

To those who tried to comfort him for the harshness of his lot, the old man would say, "Man lives a hundred years, half in days, half in nights. By day I am a common servant, and the pains of my life are as they are. But by night I am lord over men, and there is no greater satisfaction. What have I to resent?"

The mind of the clan head was occupied with worldly affairs; his attention was absorbed by his estate. Worn out in mind and body, he too was insensible with fatigue when he slept. But night after night he dreamed he was a servant, rushing and running to perform his tasks. For this he was rebuked and scolded or beaten with a stick, and he took whatever he got. He mumbled and moaned in his sleep and quieted down only with dawn's approach.

The head of the clan took his problem to a friend, who said, "Your position gives you far more wealth and honor than other men have. Your dream that you are a servant is nothing more than the cycle of comfort and hardship; this has ever been the norm of human fortune. How could you have both your dream and your waking life the same?"

The head of the clan reflected on his friend's opinion and eased the work of his servants. He also reduced his own worries, thus giving himself some relief from his dreams.

—*Lieh Tzu*

🌸 The Mortal Lord

The patriarch Ching of the land of Ch'i was with his companions on Mount Ox. As he looked northward out over his capital, tears rose in his eyes. "Such a splendid land," he said, "swarming, burgeoning; if only I didn't have to die and leave it as the waters pass! What if from the eldest times there were no death: would I ever have to leave here?"

His companions joined him in weeping. "Even for the simple fare we eat," they said, "for the nag and plank wagon we have to ride, we depend upon our lord's generosity. If *we* have no wish to die, how much less must our lord."

Yen Tzu was the only one smiling, somewhat apart. The patriarch wiped away his tears and looked hard at Yen Tzu. "These two who weep with me share the sadness I feel on today's venture," said the patriarch. "Why do you alone smile, sir?"

"What if the worthiest ruled forever?" asked Yen Tzu. "Then T'ai or Huan would be patriarch forever. What if the bravest? Then Chuang or Ling would be patriarch forever. With such as those in power, my lord, you would now be in the rice fields, wearing a straw cape and bamboo hat, careworn from digging, with no time to brood over death. And then, my lord, how could you have reached the position you now hold? It was through the succession of your predecessors, who held and vacated the throne each in his turn, that you came to be lord over this land. For you

alone to lament this is selfish. Seeing a selfish lord and his fawn-
ing, flattering subjects, I presumed to smile."

The patriarch was embarrassed, raised his flagon, and penal-
ized his companions two drafts of wine apiece.

—Lieh Tzu

◈ One Word Solves a Mystery

A member of the older generation told me this story about a shrewd magistrate in a certain county early in the dynasty.

A local merchant was about to go on a selling trip. After loading his boat, he waited on it for his servant. Time passed, but the servant did not appear. Meanwhile it occurred to the boatman that it would be easy enough in this deserted spot to do away with the merchant and steal the goods. The boatman swiftly forced the merchant into the water and drowned him. Then the murderer took the goods to his own home, after which he presented himself at the house of the merchant. He knocked on the gate and asked why the master still had not come down to the boat. The merchant's wife sent servants to look for her husband, but they saw no trace of him. She questioned the merchant's own servant, who said that he had arrived late at the boat only to find his master gone.

The family reported the matter to the local constable, who in turn informed the county officials, who then interrogated the boatman and the neighbors but uncovered no evidence. The investigation went through several levels of the bureaucracy without being settled.

When the case reached the magistrate, he sent everyone out of the room except the merchant's wife. He asked for an exact description of events at the time when the boatman first came to inquire about the merchant. "My husband had been gone a good while," said the wife, "when the boatman knocked at the gate.

Before I opened it, he suddenly cried out, 'Mistress, why hasn't the master come down yet? It's been so long.' That's all he said."

The magistrate sent the woman out and called for the boatman, who made a statement that agreed with the wife's. "That's it, then," said the magistrate with a smile. "The merchant has been killed, and you are the killer! You have confessed."

"What confession?" the boatman protested loudly.

"When you knocked at the merchant's house, you addressed his wife, not him. You did not see who was behind the gate, yet you were sure he was not at home. How else could you have known this?"

The astonished boatman confessed and was convicted.

—Chu Yün-ming

A Wise Judge

Early one morning, a grocer on his way to market to buy vegetables was surprised to find a sheaf of paper money on the ground. It was still dark, and the dealer tucked himself out of the way and waited for daylight so he could examine the money he had picked up. He counted fifteen notes worth five ounces of silver and five notes worth a string of one thousand copper coins each. Out of this grand sum he took a note, bought two strings' worth of meat and three strings' worth of hulled rice, and placed his purchases in the baskets that hung from his shoulder pole. Then he went home without buying the vegetables he had set out to buy.

When his mother asked why he had no vegetables, he replied, "I found this money early in the morning on my way to market. So I bought some meat and hulled rice and came home."

"What are you trying to put over on me?" his mother asked angrily. "If it were lost money, it couldn't be more than a note or two. How could anyone lose a whole sheaf? It's not stolen, is it? If you really found it on the ground, you should take it back."

When the son refused to follow his mother's advice, she threatened to report the matter to the officials. At that he said, "And to whom shall I return something I found on the road?"

"Go back to the place where you found the money," said his mother, "and see if the owner comes looking for it. Then you can return it to him." She added, "All our lives we've been poor. Now you've bought all this meat and rice; such sudden gains are sure to lead to misfortune."

The vegetable dealer took the notes back to where he had found them. Sure enough, someone came looking for the money.

The dealer, who was a simple country fellow, never thought to ask how much money had been lost. "Here's your money," he said and handed it over. Bystanders urged the owner to reward the finder, but the owner was such a miser that he refused, saying, "I lost thirty notes. Half the money is still missing."

With such a large difference between the amounts claimed, the argument went on and on until it was brought to court for a hearing. The county magistrate, Nieh Yi-tao, grilled the vegetable dealer and saw that his answers were basically truthful. He sent secretly for the mother, questioned her closely, and found that her answers agreed with her son's. Next he had the two disputing parties submit written statements to the court. The man who had lost money swore that he was missing thirty five-ounce bills. The vegetable dealer swore that he had found fifteen five-ounce bills.

"All right, then," said Nieh Yi-tao, "the money found is not this man's money. These fifteen bills are heaven's gift to a worthy mother to sustain her in old age." He handed the money to mother and son and told them to leave. Then he said to the man who had lost his money, "The thirty bills you lost must be in some other place. Look for them yourself." Nieh Yi-tao dismissed him with a good scolding, to the outspoken approval of all who heard it.

—*Yang Yü*

🌸 A Clever Judge

In the days when Ch'en Shu-ku was a magistrate in Chienchou, there was a man who had lost an article of some value. A number of people were arrested, but no one could discover exactly who the thief was. So Shu-ku laid a trap for the suspects. "I know of a temple," he told them, "whose bell can tell a thief from an honest man. It has great spiritual powers."

The magistrate had the bell fetched and reverently enshrined in a rear chamber. Then he had the suspects brought before the bell to stand and testify to their guilt or innocence. He explained to them that if an innocent man touched the bell it would remain silent, but that if the man was guilty it would ring out.

Then the magistrate led his staff in solemn worship to the bell. The sacrifices concluded, he had the bell placed behind a curtain, while one of his assistants secretly smeared it with ink. After a time he took the suspects to the bell and had each one in turn extend his hands through the curtain and touch the bell. As each man withdrew his hands, Shu-ku examined them. Everyone's hands were stained except for those of one man, who confessed to the theft under questioning. He had not dared touch the bell for fear it would ring.

—*Chang Shih-nan*

A Fine Phoenix

A man of Ch'u was carrying a pheasant in a cage over his shoulder. A traveler on the road said to him, "What kind of bird is that?"

"A phoenix," replied the man of Ch'u to fool the traveler.

"I've heard of such a creature, and today I'm actually seeing one! Are you selling it?"

"Yes."

The man of Ch'u declined a thousand pieces of silver for the bird, but finally accepted when the offer reached two thousand. The buyer was intending to present the bird to the king of Ch'u, but it died during the night. Although he was not too distressed over the wasted money, he keenly regretted the loss of the king's gift.

The particulars of this story became known in the state of Ch'u. It was generally assumed that the bird was a real phoenix and therefore priceless. At last the king himself learned of the intended present and was so moved that he summoned the man and rewarded him with ten times the cost of the pheasant.

—*Han-tan Shun*

Sun Tribute

"All it takes to kill a peasant is to keep him idle." So goes the proverb. Out early in the morning, home late at night—the peasant regards this as a normal life. Beans and leaves, he thinks, make a perfect meal. His skin and flesh are coarse and tough. His muscles and joints flex quickly. But put him down one day amid soft furs and silken curtains, give him fine meats and fragrant oranges, and you will see how his mind softens and his body grows restless as he suffers from fever. If a prince were to trade places with him, the prince would be exhausted in a couple of hours. Thus there is nothing better in the world than what contents and delights the peasant!

In olden days in the state of Sung, a peasant was wearing a hemp-padded garment that had barely gotten him through the winter. With the coming of spring and the toil of plowing, the man bared his back and let the sun warm his body. Unaware that there were such things in the world as grand mansions and heated rooms, cotton padding and fox fur, he turned to his wife and said, "I feel the warmth of the sun on my back, but no one knows about this great luxury. As tribute I'm going to take it to our lord, and he will give me a rich reward."

—*Lieh Tzu*

AN UNOFFICIAL
HISTORY OF
THE CONFUCIAN
ACADEMY

This tale is taken from Wu Ching-tzu's Ju Lin Wai Shih (The Scholars), a novel written in the second quarter of the eighteenth century. Wu's book, of which this story is the first chapter, is a satire on the manners and morals of the scholar officials under the Manchu (Ch'ing) Dynasty, 1644–1911.

Toward the end of the Mongol reign* there came into the world a man of towering integrity, yet frank and plain. His name? Wang Mien. His home? A village in Chuchi county in the province of Chekiang. Wang Mien's father died when he was seven, and his mother took in sewing so that the boy could study at the village school. Some three years went by this way. Then Wang Mien was ten.

Wang Mien's mother called him to her. "My dear son," she said, "I would never want to hold you back, but since Father died and left me a widow all alone, the money has been going out but not coming in. Times are hard, what with rice and kindling so dear. I have pawned or sold whatever I could of our old clothes and household goods. How can I keep you in school, when all we have is what I scrape together sewing for people? What can I do, then, but let you go to work grazing our neighbor's buffalo to make a bit of money each month? You'll get meals too, but you must go tomorrow."

"I think you're right, mother," said Wang Mien. "I was getting bored sitting in school anyway. I'd rather go and tend the buffalo; it might be a little more fun. If I want to study, I can take a few books along, the way I always do." So things were settled that very night.

Next day Wang Mien's mother went with him to their neighbors, the Ch'in family. Old Ch'in had them stay for breakfast and then led out a water buffalo, which he turned over to Wang

* The Mongols, who ruled China for three generations, were overthrown in 1368, when the Ming Dynasty was established and China once again came fully under Chinese rule. This book opens with the period just before the Mongol defeat, and the Chinese officials it portrays were later denounced as collaborators.

Mien. The farmer pointed beyond his gate and said, "Just a couple of bowshots from here you'll find Seven Lakes. Along the
lake runs a stretch of green grass where the buffalo of all the
families doze. There are dozens of good-sized willows that give
plenty of shade. When the buffalo get thirsty, they can drink at
the lakeside. Enjoy yourself there, young fellow; no need to go
far. And you'll never get less than two meals a day, plus the bit of
cash I can spare you. But you must work hard. I hope my offer
isn't disappointing."

After making her apologies, Wang Mien's mother turned to go,
and her son escorted her out the gate. Giving his clothes a last

straightening, she said, "You must be very careful here. Don't give anyone cause to find fault with you. Go out at daybreak and get home by nightfall, and spare me any worry." Wang Mien said he understood, and his mother left, holding back her tears.

From that time Wang Mien spent his days tending the Ch'in family's buffalo. At dusk he would return to his own home for the night. There were times when the Ch'ins offered him a little salted fish or preserved meat, and without fail he would wrap it in a lotus leaf and take it home to his mother. As for the few coppers he was given for snacks, he always saved them up for a month or two. Then he would steal a free moment to go to the village school and buy a few books from the bookseller there. Every day after tethering the buffalo, he would sit and read beneath the willows.

Another three or four years sped by. Wang Mien kept studying and began to see the real meaning of what he read. On one of the hottest days of midsummer when the weather was unbearable, Wang Mien was idling on the grass, tired out from tending the buffalo. Suddenly dense clouds spread across the sky. A storm came and went. Then the dark clouds fringed with white began to break, letting through a stream of sunshine that set the whole lake aglow. The hills above the lake were masses of green, blue, and purple; the trees, freshly bathed, showed their loveliest green. In the lake itself, clear water dripped from dozens of lotus buds, and beads like pearls rolled back and forth over the lotus leaves.

Wang Mien took in the scene. "Men of olden times said that man is *in* the picture," he thought. "How true! If only we had a painter with us to do a few branches of these lotuses—how fascinating it would be!" At the same time it occurred to Wang Mien:

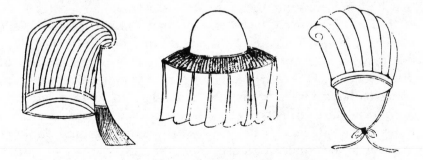

"There's nothing in the world that can't be mastered. Why not paint a few myself!"

While entertaining these daydreams, what did Wang Mien see in the distance but a clumsy porter shouldering a load of food suspended from a pole and carrying a jug of wine in his hand. A mat was draped over the packages of food. When he arrived under the willows, he spread the mat and opened up the packages. From the same direction three men were approaching who wore scholars' mortarboards on their heads. One of them was dressed in the sapphire-blue robe of a degree holder, the other two simply in dark robes. All three appeared to be forty or fifty years old. They advanced with leisurely step, fanning themselves with white paper fans.

The one in blue was a fat man. When he arrived beneath the willows he showed one of his companions, who had a beard, to the place of honor and the other, a skinny man, to a place opposite. The fat man must have been the host, for he took the lowest seat and poured the wine. After they had spent some time eating, the fat man opened his mouth to speak: "Old Master Wei is back! He just bought a new house. It's even bigger than the one he had in the capital and cost two thousand taels of silver! Because Master Wei was the buyer, the owner lowered the price a few dozen taels for the sake of the prestige that would rub off on him. Master Wei moved into the house early last month. Their Honors, the governor and the county magistrate, came personally to his door to offer their congratulations and were entertained there until well into the night. The whole city holds him in the highest regard."

"His Honor the county magistrate," said the skinny man, "won his penultimate degree in the triennial examination. Master Wei was his examiner, hence his patron. So it was only to be expected that he would come to congratulate his patron."

"My brother-in-law," said the fat man, "is also Master Wei's protégé. Now he's a county magistrate in Honan province. Day before yesterday my son-in-law brought over a few pounds of dried venison. (There it is on the plate.) When he returns, I'm going to have him ask my brother-in-law to write a letter to introduce me to Master Wei. If Master Wei honors us with a return visit, our fields will be saved from the pigs and donkeys that our local farmers let loose to eat their fill."

"Old Master Wei's a true scholar!" said the skinny man.

"They say that when he left the capital a few days ago," added the bearded man, "the emperor himself saw him out to the city wall, and then they walked about a dozen steps hand in hand. Master Wei had to bow down again and again declining the honor, before His Majesty returned to his sedan-chair. The way things look, Master Wei should soon be in office." Thus the conversation went back and forth, never reaching an end. Wang Mien, however, saw that evening was approaching, so he hauled his charge home.

Now Wang Mien no longer put the money he saved into books. Instead he had someone buy him some pigments and white lead powder so that he could learn to paint the lotus. His first efforts were not especially good, but after a few months he could make a perfect likeness of the blossom both in outward appearance and essential quality. Had it not been for the sheet of paper they were on, his lotuses could be growing in the lake! Some local people who saw how well he painted even paid money for his work, and with it Wang bought a few treats for his mother.

Word spread until the whole county of Chuchi knew that there was among them a master of brushwork in the "boneless" or soft-shape style of flower painting. People began competing to buy the paintings. When Wang Mien reached the age of seventeen or eighteen, he was no longer working for the Ch'in family. Every day he would make a few sketches or study the ancient poets. As time went by he did not have to worry about food or clothing, and his mother was happy as could be.

Wang Mien was so gifted that before he was twenty he had mastered such fields of knowledge as astronomy, geography, the classics, and the historical texts. But he was unusual in that he sought neither office nor friends; he remained secluded with his studies. When he saw illustrations of Ch'ü Yüan's* costume in an edition of Ch'ü's great poem "Li Sao," Wang Mien fitted himself out with the same kind of tall tablet-like hat and billowing robe.

When the season of fair days arrived, he set his mother in a bullock cart, garbed himself after his newest fashion, and with a whip in his hand and a song on his lips, traveled around wherever

* One of China's most famous statesman-poets, he lived in the late fourth to early third centuries, b.c. When his king did not accept his principled advice, he drowned himself in the Milo River in Hunan.

it pleased him—to the neighboring villages and towns or down to the lakeside. His jaunts excited the laughter of the village children, who tagged after him in little groups. Wang Mien did not care. Only Old Ch'in, his neighbor, loved and respected him, for though the old man was a farmer, he had a mind of his own and had seen Wang Mien grow from youth to cultivated maturity. Time and again the two enjoyed the warmest companionship when he invited Wang Mien to his cottage.

One day when Wang Mien was visiting with Old Ch'in, what did they see outside but a man coming toward them—a man wearing the conelike cap and black cotton of a lowly officer. Old Ch'in welcomed the visitor, and after mutual courtesies the two men sat down. The visitor's surname was Chai, and he was serving the Chuchi county magistrate as chief sergeant and steward at the same time. Since the eldest of Old Ch'in's sons was a ward of Steward Chai's and called him Godfather, the steward frequently came down to the village to visit his relative.

Old Ch'in made a big fuss and told his son to brew tea, kill a chicken, and cook up some meat to entertain Chai in grand style. Then he asked Wang Mien to join them. After Old Ch'in introduced Wang Mien to his guest, Steward Chai said, "Can this honorable Mr. Wang be the expert painter of flowers in the soft-shape style?"

"The very man himself," replied Old Ch'in. "But my dear relative, however did you know?"

"Who around town doesn't?" said the steward. "A few days ago His Honor, our county magistrate, told me he wants a folio of twenty-four flower paintings to send to *his* superior and turned the job over to me. People speak so highly of Wang Mien that I came especially to you, dear relative. And now fortune enables me to meet Mr. Wang, whom I would trouble for a few strokes of his honored brush. In a fortnight I shall return here to fetch them. I am sure His Honor will have a few taels of silver to 'moisten the brush'; I'll be bringing them along."

From the sidelines Old Ch'in was earnestly prodding Wang Mien who, rather than hurt Old Ch'in's feelings, had no choice but to accept. He went home and threw himself into the composition of the twenty-four floral pieces, adding a poem to each. The steward Chai reported to his office, and the magistrate Shih Jen paid out twenty-four taels of silver. The steward took twelve taels for his commission, delivered twelve to Wang Mien and left with the folio. The magistrate took the folio from the steward and assembled a few other gifts for Mr. Wei to wish him well.

Wei Su was interested in none of the gifts except the folio. He cherished it, savored it, would not let it out of his hands. The next day he invited Magistrate Shih to a banquet at his home to express his thanks. And there they passed the time of day as the wine went round.

"A day ago I received the flower album Your Honor so kindly sent," said Wei Su. "I wonder, is it the work of some classic master or a man of our own times?"

The magistrate could hardly keep the truth from his superior. "The painter is a local peasant from your protégé's district. His name is Wang Mien, and he is quite young—just a beginner. He hardly deserves to come within your discerning view, dear patron."

"Humble student that I am," said Wei Su with a sigh, "I have been away so long that I am guilty of ignorance that so worthy a talent has come from my home village. A shame. A shame. This good fellow has not only the highest skill but a wealth of knowledge. Most unusual! He will equal us one day in name and in position, too. Could you arrange for me to meet with him, I wonder?"

"No problem," replied the magistrate. "When I leave I shall have someone arrange it. When Wang Mien learns that it is my dear patron who takes such an interest in him, I know he will be beside himself with delight." And with that he bid adieu to Wei Su, returned to his office, and assigned the steward Chai to invite Wang Mien in the humblest and most courteous form to a meeting with Wei Su.

The steward fairly flew to the village and went straight to the home of Old Ch'in to present the invitation. And if he presented it to Wang Mien five times, he presented it to him ten times, but Wang Mien only laughed and said, "I'm sorry, but I shall have to trouble you, Steward, to report back to His Honor that Wang Mien is a mere peasant who would never dream of such an audience. Nor would I dream of accepting this invitation."

The steward's face darkened as he said, "Who would dare refuse His Honor's invitation? Not to mention the fact that if I myself hadn't done you the favor, His Honor would never have known of your talent. It stands to reason that after meeting His Honor, you should find a way to show me your gratitude. And what's the idea of not putting out a cup of tea for me after I've come all this way? And giving me this excuse and that for being unwilling to go—what's it supposed to mean? And how am I supposed to make a proper report to His Honor? Are you trying to tell me that the head of a whole county can't summon a commoner?"

"Steward," said Wang Mien, "there's something you don't understand. If I had done something wrong and His Honor issued an official summons for my appearance, how could I refuse? But this is only an invitation, which means he's not *demanding* that I go. I'd rather not go. His Honor should forgive me!"

"What in hell are you talking about?" said the steward. "You'll go if you're summoned, but not if you're invited? You don't appreciate it when someone tries to help you!"

"Good Mr. Wang, okay, okay," said Old Ch'in. "If His Honor sends an invitation, of course he means well. Why not go this time with my dear relative? You know the saying, 'A magistrate can ruin the family.' Why be so stubborn?"

"Uncle," said Wang Mien, "the steward doesn't know this, but haven't you heard me tell of ancient worthies who refused their sovereign's call? I really won't go."

"You present me with a difficult problem," said the steward. "What explanation can I take back to His Honor?"

"This is a real dilemma," said Old Ch'in, "between going and not going. On the one hand, Mr. Wang refuses to go; on the other, my dear relative will be hard put to explain it if he doesn't. However, I may have a way out. When you return to the city, dear relative, don't say that Mr. Wang won't go, only that he is ill at home and cannot come right away, but will in a few days when he's feeling better."

"I'd need four neighbors to vouch for that!" cried the steward. And so they argued round and round. Old Ch'in made supper for the steward and quietly told Wang to bring half a tael of silver from his mother, to reimburse the steward for his travel expenses.

When Magistrate Shih heard the steward's report, he thought, "How could the rascal have taken ill? This lackey of a steward must have gone into the village like 'the fox in front of the tiger'* and scared the life out of the artist, who has probably never yet been received by an official. But since my patron, Wei Su, has left it to me to arrange a meeting, he will hold me in contempt if I

* See "The Tiger Behind the Fox," page 67.

flunk this test. It appears that I'll have to pay my respects to the artist personally. This gracious compliment, with no hint of coercion, will surely give him the courage to meet me, and then I'll take him along to see my patron. In that way I can pass the test with distinction!"

But the magistrate had another thought: "For a county magistrate to lower himself to pay his respects to a peasant will provoke the scorn of his underlings."

Then the magistrate had yet another thought: "The other day my patron spoke of this artist with one hundred percent respect. I, therefore, should be one thousand percent respectful. Besides, if I lower myself to show respect to a worthy peasant, the local chronicles will surely include a section in praise of it—to my eternal credit! I can't see anything wrong in that!" And so the magistrate made his decision.

Next morning he called for his sedan-chair. Dispensing with the full complement of heralds and banners, he took only eight guards to clear the road ahead, as well as the steward Chai, who hung onto the rails of the sedan-chair. They went directly to the village. When the villagers heard the gong announcing an official's approach, they came crowding forth to look, supporting their elderly and taking their young by the hand.

The chair arrived at Wang Mien's gate. And what did the steward find? Seven or eight thatched-roof huts and an unpainted wooden door, tightly shut. The steward bounded up to the door. After he had knocked at it for a while, an old woman came out, propped herself up on her walking stick, and said, "Wang Mien's not home. He took the buffalo to water first thing this morning and he hasn't returned yet."

"His Honor has come himself to summon your son," said the steward. "What are you wasting time for? Tell me where he is right away, so that I can deliver the summons."

"The simple truth," said the old woman, "is that he's not here, and I don't know where he has gone." With that she went back inside, closing the door behind her.

While they had been talking, the magistrate's chair pulled up. The steward kneeled before it and offered his report: "Your humble servant has been trying to summon Wang Mien, but he is not at home. May I suggest, Your Honor, that you have your dragon-chair moved to the public rest house, while I continue my efforts." With steward Chai hanging on as before, the chair was carried behind Wang Mien's cottage, where there was a jumble of raised footpaths bordering the fields. Beyond them was a large pond bordered with elms and mulberries. Farther in the distance stretched an expanse of acres. There was a small hill too, near the pond, green with dense foliage. It stood about half a mile from Wang Mien's house, and two people could hail one another from hill to house.

As the magistrate was being carried away, a water buffalo with a cowherd riding it backwards came from behind the hill. The steward hurried over to him and asked, "Young man, did you see where your neighbor Wang Mien took his animal?"

"You mean Uncle Wang?" answered the second of Old Ch'in's sons. "He's off to a feast in the Wang clan's hamlet—about seven miles from here. But this is his buffalo. He asked me to drive it home."

The steward informed the magistrate, who scowled. "If that's the case," he said, "there's no point in my going to the rest house. We will return to the office at once." By this time the magistrate was so angry that his first thought was to have Wang Mien arrested and taught a painful lesson. But on second thought he was afraid that his patron would criticize him for being hot-tempered. It might be better to hold his peace and explain that Wang Mien was not worth doing a favor. The young peasant himself could be dealt with in good time. With these thoughts the magistrate left the village.

Wang Mien had not in fact gone far at all, and soon he came strolling home. Thoroughly annoyed, Old Ch'in came up to him and said, "You were altogether too willful just now. He is the head of the whole county. How could you be so insolent?"

"Good sir," said Wang Mien, "please sit down. I have something to tell you. The magistrate, backed by Wei Su's power, has been maltreating our peasants every way he can. Why should I have anything to do with such a person? The thing is that when he goes back he's sure to say something to Wei Su. If Wei Su takes offense at the insult, he'll be looking to settle scores with me, I'm afraid. So for now I'll bid you goodbye, get my things together, and go away to keep out of trouble, though leaving my mother alone at home makes me uneasy."

"Son," said Wang Mien's mother, "you have been selling your art work for years. Out of that I've saved forty or fifty taels of silver. So I won't be wanting for the basics. And though I'm old,

my health is good. I can't see any reason why you shouldn't get out of the way for a while. Besides, you haven't committed any crime. The officers aren't going to come and take me away!"

"She has a point," said Old Ch'in. "Moreover, your talents will go unrecognized buried in this village town. Take yourself off to some important place where you may meet your fortune. As for your most honorable mother—I'll be responsible for everything at home while you're gone." Wang Mien thanked Old Ch'in with clasped hands upraised. The farmer went back to his house to fetch some wine and delicacies, and with these he bid a fitting farewell to Wang Mien. They spent half the night celebrating before Old Ch'in went home.

The next day before dawn, Wang Mien got up and collected his things. Old Ch'in arrived as he was finishing breakfast. Wang Mien bid his mother a respectful goodbye, and mother and son, shedding tears, parted hands. Wang Mien slipped on his hemp shoes, set his pack on his back, and went to the village entrance. Carrying a small white lantern, Old Ch'in accompanied him. The two men wept. Old Ch'in, lantern in hand, stood watching Wang Mien until he was out of sight.

Exposed to the elements, stopping every twenty or thirty miles at hostels, Wang Mien traveled straight to the city of Tsinan, capital of Shantung. Though Shantung is a northern, hence a poorer, province, Tsinan is populous and prosperous. When Wang Mien arrived his money had all been spent, so he had to rent a small dwelling attached to the front of a convent. There he read the stars and told people's fortunes. He also painted a few soft-shape lotus blossoms, which he put up for sale to passersby. His work was so popular that he could not keep the crowds away.

Snap your fingers; half a year passed. There were some vulgar plutocrats in the city who prized Wang Mien's pictures and were always eager to buy them. Of course these wealthy men did not come personally; they sent their lackeys, who shouted and called out orders and made such a commotion that Wang Mien had no peace. When he could bear it no longer, he painted a huge ox and pasted it up together with some barbed verses. He knew this would lead to trouble and began thinking about moving on.

One day in the clear early dawn he was sitting in his room when he was amazed to see a great crowd of men and women shrieking and wailing as they moved down the street. In the baskets that hung from their shoulder poles, some had pots and household things and some had children. All were gaunt and ragged. They streamed past, rank after rank, filling up the street. Some sat on the ground and begged. Asked why they were here, they said they had come from the shires and counties along the Yellow River. Their fields and homes had been swept away, they said, when the river broke through the dikes and flooded the countryside. They were ordinary folk fleeing a disaster for which the government had no concern. So they could only take to the road to survive.

Wang Mien could not stand to watch them. "The river is overflowing north," he said with a sigh, "and the world enters a period of great disorder. What's the point in remaining here?" He gathered up what money he had, tied his things together in a bundle, and went back home. It was only when he reached the border of his home province that he learned Wei Su was back in the capital and the magistrate had been promoted. So it was safe to return home and pay respects to his mother.

He was glad to find her hale as ever. She told him of the many kindnesses Old Ch'in had shown her. Quickly unpacking, Wang Mien took a bolt of silk and some dried persimmon to Old Ch'in to show his gratitude. The farmer prepared a homecoming celebration, and afterwards Wang Mien chanted poems, made pictures, and took care of his mother as he had done before.

Six years went by. Wang Mien's mother, now old and unwell, kept to her bed. Wang Mien tried every kind of cure and doctor—to no avail. One day his mother gave him the following advice: "I can see that I am past saving. Now, these few years people have been bending my ears saying that since you are so learned I should encourage you to go and become an official. No doubt that would reflect well on your ancestors. And yet these officials never seem to come to a good end. With your proud spirit, the outcome would be dreadful if you got yourself in trouble. So my son, heed these last words—take a wife and raise a family; care for my grave—and don't become an official. That way I can die in peace, eyes and mouth closed."

Wang Mien tearfully assented. His mother drew her last few soft breaths and went home to the heavens. The grieving son pounded his bosom and stamped his feet and gave voice to his sorrow, and his cries moved the neighbors to tears. He asked Old Ch'in to help prepare the burial clothes and the coffin. Wang Mien himself carried the earth to make the grave mound, and for the required twenty-five months he "slept on earth and hemp" in mourning.

Hardly a year after the ceremonial mourning ended, a great revolution broke out. The anti-Mongol leader Fang Kuo-chen seized Chekiang province, Chang Shih-ch'eng seized Suchou, and Ch'en Yu-liang seized the Hupei-Hunan region. But these three were only bandit-heroes. The founder of the Ming Dynasty was to be Chu Yüan-chang,* the Great Imperial Ancestor, who raised an army at Chuyang, captured Nanking, and established himself as the king of Wu. His righteous legions smashed the bandit-hero Fang Kuo-chen and gave him command of all Chekiang, and the villages and towns knew peace.

One day at noon as Wang Mien was returning home after the ceremonial sweeping of his mother's grave, he was surprised to

* When the Ming Dynasty was established in 1368, it ended over two and a half centuries of political dominance by non-Chinese. In 1644 the non-Chinese Manchu dynasty, the Ch'ing, was established. It fell in the Republican Revolution of 1911. This novel was written toward the middle of the eighteenth century, that is, at the height of Manchu rule, when Ming loyalism was regarded as sedition.

see a dozen horsemen heading into his village. The man in the lead wore an army cap on his head and a military tunic. With his light, clear face and three-strand whiskers, he had the marks of a true Chinese sovereign. The man dismounted at Wang Mien's gate, greeted him courteously, and said, "May I trouble you with a question? Where is the home of Master Wang Mien?"

"Your humble servant," replied Wang Mien. "This poor home is mine."

"Marvelous," said the man, "for it is you I come to greet." He ordered his men to dismount, picket their horses by the lakeside willows, and take up posts outside the cottage. The leader alone took Wang Mien by the hands and went with him indoors, where they seated themselves as host and guest and exchanged further amenities.

Wang Mien said, "I dare not inquire your most respected name and title and why you have favored this remote village with a visit."

"I am named Chu," replied the man. "I have raised armies throughout southeast China and previously held the title king of Chuyang. Now that I have taken Nanking, I am known as the king of Wu.* I have come to conquer the forces of the bandit-hero Fang Kuo-chen, and wish in particular to pay my respects to you."

"Oh! Simple villager that I am, to lack the eyes to see! So it's really Your Highness! How dare a foolish peasant take Your Grace out of his way?"

"This poor orphan,"† said the king of Wu, "is a crude, rough fellow. But now that I see your air of learning, my thoughts of worldly fame and merit seem to vanish. All during my campaigns I have held your name in esteem. Today I come to pay respectful call in hopes of receiving your instruction, Master. Since the people of Chekiang have long been in rebellion, what can be done to win their hearts and minds?"

"Needless for a peasant to tell it to a man of enlightenment and foresight like Your Majesty," replied Wang Mien. "If the basic principles of humanity and rectitude be used to win the people's loyalty, who in the whole world could hold out against you? If you conquer our weak people by force, their sense of rectitude

---

* Wu was an ancient name for southeast China.

† This was the conventional way for a Chinese king to refer to himself.

will keep them from the disgrace of submission. Look what happened to Fang Kuo-chen!"

The king of Wu sighed deeply and nodded in approval, and the two spoke together until the sun went down. The king's followers had brought dry rations of cooked grain with them, and Wang Mien went himself to the kitchen to bake a good helping of cakes and fry up a plate of leeks. He served the king and then joined him for the supper, after which the king thanked Wang Mien for his wise advice and left on horseback.

The same day Old Ch'in returned from town and asked about the visitor. But Wang Mien never said exactly who had come, only that it was an army officer with whom he had made friends when he was in Shantung.

A few years later the king of Wu calmed the catastrophic turmoil in the world and reestablished the sacred cauldron in Nanking—symbol of the continuity of the most ancient dynastic heritage. The realm was united. The new dynasty was called Great Ming, and the emperor's reign title was "Overwhelming Might." All over the land the peasantry worked in peace and contentment.

In the fourth year of Overwhelming Might, Old Ch'in went into the city and returned to tell Wang Mien, "His Honor Wei Su has answered for his crimes and has been sent into exile. I brought a copy of the whole notice to show you." Thus Wang Mien learned that after surrendering to the Ming forces, Wei Su had claimed that he had been the new emperor's loyal vassal all along. The emperor was so furious that he exiled Wei Su to Hochou, where he was assigned to tend the tomb of a famous general of the Mongol reign.

Another document that Old Ch'in brought back was the regulations of the Board of Rites governing the selection of officials. As before, there would be an examination requiring formal essays on the Confucian classics every third year. "Actually," said Wang Mien, "these rules are awful. Whenever scholars have this route to fame and glory, they do not take a serious approach to the correct principles for composition, conduct, official service, and seclusion."

As they spoke evening came on. It was early summer, and the weather was unexpectedly warm. Old Ch'in set out a table in a clearing for threshing wheat, and the two men enjoyed a supper with a little wine. Then the moon stole up from the east, making everything glisten like an endless expanse of glass. Not a sound came from the sleeping seagulls and resting cormorants. Wang Mien held his cup in his left hand and pointed to the stars with his right. "Look," he said, "the constellation Shackles will cross Literary Splendor. Things will not go smoothly for this generation of scholars."

As Wang Mien was speaking, a sudden wind sprang up and knifed through the trees with an ominous hiss, scaring the water-fowl into croaking flight. Old Ch'in and Wang Mien covered their faces in fear. But soon the wind died down, and when they opened their eyes they saw something amazing: hundreds of little stars were streaming from every direction down toward the southeast corner of the sky. "Heaven may have pity on us yet," said Wang Mien, "sending down this troop of star-princes to maintain the fortunes of the scholars—but not in our lifetimes." They cleared the table and went separately home.

From then on, talk was heard that the Ming government had sent orders to the Chekiang governor to draft Wang Mien into the ranks of officials. At first Wang Mien did not take the rumors seriously, but the talk only increased. And so, without telling Old Ch'in, Wang Mien quietly gathered his belongings and slipped away by night to the K'uaichi Mountains.

Half a year later the Ming court actually sent an official with an imperial summons. He was attended by many men and brought splendid gifts. He arrived at Old Ch'in's gate and found a man now past eighty years of age, his beard and sideburns silvery white, hands gripping a staff. The imperial messenger extended his courtesies and Old Ch'in ushered him into the cottage. "Is Master Wang Mien in this hamlet?" the messenger asked. "The Imperial Grace grants him the office of Consulting Military Adviser. I have come expressly to present the imperial written command."

"He's from our village," replied Old Ch'in, "but it's been a long time since I knew his whereabouts." Old Ch'in offered some tea and then led the official to Wang Mien's home. He pushed open the gate. Spiders and webs filled the rooms; brambles and weeds covered the paths. The official could see for himself that Wang Mien had been gone a long time. With a sad sigh, the messenger took his document back to the capital to report on his mission.

Wang Mien lived in obscurity in the K'uaichi Mountains, taking care never to reveal his identity. Some time later, he took sick and passed on. His neighbors collected a little money and buried him at the foot of the mountains. That same year Old Ch'in also reached his mortal term. It's strange, but these days writers and scholars speak of Wang Mien as Consulting Military Adviser, though in all honesty, when did he serve in office even for a single day? That's why I have tried to set the record straight.

—Wu Ching-tzu

 # Nature

The ground is held in place by the major mountains. It has the rocks for bones, the rivers for veins, and the vegetation for its coat. Its flesh is the earth—the top two and a half feet of soil that things grow in. Beneath lies the ground itself.

—Chang Hua

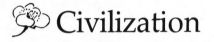 Civilization

In the southern corner of the extreme west is the great primitive grassland surrounded by lands unknown. There the vital forces of the universe, the *yin* and the *yang*, do not interchange, so there is no contrast of heat and cold. No light of sun or moon shines on it, so there is neither day nor night. The people do not eat or wear clothes but sleep most of the time, waking only once every fifty days. They believe that what they do in their dreams is real and what they do when awake is unreal.

The focal point within the four seas is our middle kingdom of China. Straddling the Yellow River north and south and extending over the Tai Mountains east and west, it contains many thousands of square miles. Its measure of *yin* and *yang* has been carefully determined, so it has equal seasons of cold and heat. The division of light and dark has been made with discernment, so there is equal day and night. Its people vary in intelligence. All things grow and multiply. All manner of talents and skills are found there. A king and his officers preside over them. Tradition and law sustain them. Their world is full of any number of things! They sleep and wake in regular order. They regard what they do when awake as real and what they see in dreams as unreal.

In the northern corner of the extreme east there is a land called the hill settlements, where the climate is habitually punishing. The sun and moon stay close to the horizon, and their light is weak. Most crops do not grow in the soil. The people live on roots and legumes and are ignorant of cooking. They are hard and ruthless by nature, and the stronger exploit the weaker. They honor superior force, not social ethics. Most of the time they are on the move and rarely rest. And they are always awake; they do not sleep at all.

—*Lieh Tzu*

A Note on the Translation and Transcription of Chinese

The selection and arrangement of the tales drawn from the following sources was done by the editor. All the translations were made by the editor with the assistance of C. N. Tay. A number of these tales have never before been translated into English, and most of the others are scattered in books now out of print or difficult to obtain.

The translating was done in two stages. First, an extremely literal version was made in an attempt to reproduce as faithfully as possible not only semantic nuances but also syntactical and rhythmic patterns. The second stage involved making, as sparingly as possible, adjustments of diction and style in an effort to achieve maximum readability. In addition, brief explanatory phrases have occasionally been brought into the text, factual information (dates, names, places) at the beginning of some tales has been simplified, and in a few cases a redundantly didactic ending has been abbreviated or omitted.

Because the material is classical, not modern, the Wade-Giles system of transcription has been used. Place names, which usually have two syllables, are spelled as one word: Chinling, Tungan. A state name usually has one syllable: Ch'i, Sung. Dynasties always have one: T'ang, Ming. Names of people are written with the last name first, and the first name hyphenated, if in two syllables: Tu Tzu-ch'un, Hsi Fang-p'ing. If the first name has one syllable: Liang Hsü, Hsüeh Wei. Only rarely does the last name have two syllables: Ssu-ma Ch'ien.

Vowels and diphthongs in Chinese are constant and easy to learn: *a* as in f*a*r; *ai* as in Th*ai*; *ao* as in M*ao*; *e* as in h*e*r; *ei* as in w*ei*gh; *i* as in mar*i*ne (*i* is sometimes written *yi* to avoid confusion with the English first-person pronoun I); *ih* like the *irr* in wh*irr*; *o* as in do*o*r; *ou* as in *owe*; *u* as in fl*u*te; *ü* is an *i* pronounced with rounded lips.

Initial consonants may require a little explanation. *p'*, *t'*, *k'*, *ch'*, and *ts'* come before vowels with a strong puff of breath: *p'* as in *p*ooh; *t'* as in *t*attle; *k'* as in *kh*aki; *ch'* as in *ch*alk; *ts'* as in lo*ts* of. When pronounced without the strong puff or breath, these sounds are written without the ': *p* as in s*p*ot; *t* as in s*t*all; *k* as in s*k*y; ch like the *g* in *g*em; *ts* is like the *ds* in wor*ds*; *j* at the beginning of a word resembles the final *ih* mentioned above. (Again the *rr* of whi*rr* is a close approximation, but the lips are not rounded as they always are to pronounce the English *r*.) *hs* is the same as *sh*, coming only before *i* and *ü*. Thus, *hsi* sounds like *she* with the lips retracted.

Other initial consonants and the final consonants are pronounced as in English.

List of Sources

The following list gives (1) the English title in this edition; (2) in parentheses, the Chinese title or titles in transcription, if the original has any; (3) the source or sources; and (4) the dynasty and in most cases the approximate date for the work.

The Cricket (Ts'u Chih), Liao Chai Chih I (hereafter LCCI), early Ch'ing, late 17th century A.D.

The Waiting Maid's Parrot (Ch'in Chi Liao), Ying Ch'üan I Ts'ao, Ch'ing, late 18th century A.D.

Sea Prince (Hai Kung Tzu), LCCI

A Girl in Green (Lü I Nü), LCCI

Butterfly Dreams, Chuang Tzu, Chan Kuo period, 4th century B.C.

Suited to Be a Fish (Hsüeh Wei/Yü Fu Chi), Hsü Hsüan Kuai Lu (hereafter HHKL), late T'ang, early 9th century A.D.

Li Ching and the Rain God (Li Wei Kung Ching), HHKL

Jade Leaves, Lieh Tzu, Chin, late 3rd–early 4th centuries A.D.

The Wizard's Lesson (Tu Tzu-ch'un), HHKL

The Priest of Hardwork Mountains (Lao Shan Tao Shih), LCCI

White Lotus Magic (Pai Lien Chiao), LCCI

The Peach Thief (T'ou T'ao), LCCI

The Magic Pear Tree (Chung Li), LCCI

The Wine Well (Hsin Kao), Hsüeh T'ao Hsiao Shuo from Chiu Hsiao Shuo, Ming

Gold, Gold, Lieh Tzu

Stump Watching, Han Fei Tzu, Chan Kuo period, 3rd century B.C.

Buying Shoes, Han Fei Tzu

The Missing Axe, Lieh Tzu

Overdoing It, Chan Kuo Ts'e, Chan Kuo period, 5th to 3rd centuries B.C.

The Horsetrader, Chan Kuo Ts'e

The Silver Swindle (Ch'i P'ien), Hsin Ch'i Hsieh from Li Tai Hsiao Shuo Pi Chi Hsüan, Ch'ing, late 18th century A.D.

The Family's Fortune (Wang Hsin), Hsüeh T'ao Hsiao Shuo

The Leaf, Hsiao Lin, San Kuo, Wei, 220–265 A.D.

The Tiger Behind the Fox, Chan Kuo Ts'e

Rich Man of Sung, Han Fei Tzu

The Flying Bull (Niu Fei), LCCI

Social Connections (Lien Kuei Ku Huo), Shan Chai K'o T'an, Ch'ing

A Small Favor (Ting Ch'ien-hsi), LCCI

Pitted Loquats (Wu He P'i Pa), Ch'iu Teng Ts'ung Hua, Ch'ing

Memory Trouble (Ping Wang), Ai Tzu Hou Yü from Chiu Hsiao Shuo, Ming

Medical Techniques (I Shu), LCCI

The Lost Horse, Huai Han, Tzu, early Han 2nd century B.C.

The Deer in the Dream, Lieh Tzu

Loss of Memory, Lieh Tzu

The Sun, Lieh Tzu

A Faithful Mouse (I Shu), LCCI

The Loyal Dog (I Ch'üan), LCCI

Black and White, Lieh Tzu

The Dog Goes to Court (I Ch'üan Chi), Yü Ch'u Hsin Chih, Ch'ing

The Tale of the Trusty Tiger (I Hu Chi), Chiu Hsiao Shuo, Ch'ing

The Repentant Tiger of Chaoch'eng (Chao Ch'eng Hu), LCCI

Tiger Boys (Hua Hu Chi), Yü Ch'u Hsin Chih

Human Bait (I Jen Wei Ni), Hsin Ch'i Hsieh

Educated Frogs and Martial Ants (Ha Ma Chiao Shu I P'ai Chen), Hsin Ch'i Hsieh

The Snakeman (She Jen), LCCI

The North Country Wolf (Chung Shan Lang), Tung T'ien Man Kao, Ming

Counselor to the Wolves (Lang Chün Shih), Hsin Ch'i Hsieh

Monkey Keeper, Lieh Tzu

Man and Beast, Lieh Tzu

Man or Beast, Lieh Tzu

The Fish Rejoice, Chuang Tzu

Wagging My Tail in the Mud, Chuang Tzu

Li Chi Slays the Serpent, Sou Shen Chi, Chin

The Black General (Kuo Yüan-chen/Wu Chiang Chün), Hsüan Kuai Lu, late T'ang

The Master and the Serving Maid (Liu Ch'ing), Luan Yang Hsü Lu from Chiu Hsiao Shuo, Ch'ing

A Cure for Jealousy (I Chi), Hsin Ch'i Hsieh

The Fortune Teller (Suan Ming Te Tzu), Cho Keng Lu from Li Tai Hsiao Shuo Pi Chi Hsüan, Yüan

A Dead Son, Lieh Tzu

The Golden Toothpick (Chin Pi Tz'u Jou), Cho Keng Lu

The King's Favorite, Han Fei Tzu

The Divided Daughter (Li Hun Chi), T'ang Jen Hsiao Shuo, late T'ang

The Scholar's Concubine (Kung-sun Hsia), LCCI

Three Former Lives (San Sheng), LCCI

The Monk from Everclear (Ch'ang Ch'ing Seng), LCCI

The Monk's Sins (Seng Nieh), LCCI

The Truth About Ghosts (Ch'en Tsai-heng), Chin Hu Ch'i Mo, Ch'ing

Sung Ting-po Catches a Ghost (Sung Ting-po Cho Kuei), Sou Shen Chi, Chin

The Man Who Couldn't Catch a Ghost (Kuei Pi Chiang San-mang), Yüeh Wei Ts'ao T'ang, Ch'ing

Ai Tzu and the Temple Ghost, Ai Tzu Tsa Shuo, Sung

Escaping Ghosts (Yü Ssu Pi Kuei), Ch'i Hsiu Lei Kao, Ming

Test of Conviction, Sou Shen Chi

Drinking Companions (Wang Liu-lang), LCCI

The Censor and the Tiger (Li Cheng), Hsüan Shih Chih, late T'ang

Underworld Justice (Hsi Fang-p'ing), LCCI

Sharp Sword (K'uai Tao), LCCI

The Skull, Chuang Tzu

The Sheep Butcher and His King, Chuang Tzu

The Prime Minister's Coachman, Shih Chi, early Han

The Royal Jewel, Shih Chi

Country of Thieves, Shih Chi

Strategy, Tso Chuan, Spring and Autumn period, fifth century B.C.

Buying Loyalty, Chan Kuo Ts'e

The Groom's Crimes, Yen Tzu Ch'un Ch'iu, Spring and Autumn period

The Chain, Shuo Yüan, early Han

Hearsay, Lieh Tzu

Dreams, Lieh Tzu

The Mortal Lord, Lieh Tzu

One Word Solves a Mystery (P'ien Yen Che Yü), Chih Shan Ch'ien Wen from Chiu Hsiao Shuo, Ming

A Wise Judge (Nieh Yi-tao), Shan Chü Hsin Hua from Chiu Hsiao Shuo, Yüan

A Clever Judge (Ch'en Shu-ku), Meng Chi Pi T'an, Sung

A Fine Phoenix, Hsiao Lin, San Kuo, Wei

Sun Tribute, Lieh Tzu

An Unofficial History of the Confucian Academy, chapter 1 of the Ju Lin Wai Shih, Ch'ing

Nature, Po Wu Chih, Chin

Civilization, Lieh Tzu

Index of Tales

About the Translator

Moss Roberts is Associate Professor of Chinese and Director of East Asian Studies at New York University. He received his Ph.D. from Columbia University and also did advanced work in the Oriental Languages Department at Berkeley. He is the author of several articles on Chinese philosophy and philology, and has translated *Mao Zedong's Critique of Soviet Economics* and the epic drama *Three Kingdoms*.